F...
Pa...

Liam,

You have been more like a son to me than a grandson, but now you disappoint me. Did you think I wouldn't discover your…association with Aubrey Holt? Consorting with the enemy's daughter. More than anyone, you should know the danger in such a foolish dalliance.

Holt isn't like our other competitors. He uses underhanded tactics and wouldn't hesitate to use his own daughter. Be careful, Liam. When you sleep in the viper's pit, you open yourself up to his bite.

That is not a risk I am willing to take for EPH, a company I've built with my own sweat and blood. EPH is mine, Liam, and you work for *me*. Now I'm giving you one clear direction to follow: End it with Aubrey Holt. End it—or face the consequences.

Patrick

Elliott Publication Holdings
New York

Dear Reader,

I love continuity stories, not only because they give me an opportunity to be a part of a larger project, but also because I get to "play" with fellow authors. The collaborations are a guaranteed good time and a learning experience.

This series was especially important to me because not long ago I lost a friend to breast cancer. So get 'em checked, girls.

For this particular story I got to have fun with a forbidden relationship and to revisit old friends from a previous continuity. That meant the Ashton continuity's authors gave me updates on where they thought their characters would be one year later. And because I've had several fan letters asking the sex of Mercedes Ashton—Maxwell's baby—you'll meet the little darling in this book.

I hope you enjoy a little taboo romance and a return visit to Napa Valley.

Best,

Emilie Rose

EMILIE ROSE

FORBIDDEN MERGER

Published by Silhouette Books

America's Publisher of Contemporary Romance

Special thanks and acknowledgment are given to Emilie Rose for her contribution to THE ELLIOTTS miniseries.

Thanks to Melissa Jeglinski for always providing a fun challenge and for letting me play with old friends.

And special thanks to Sheri WhiteFeather for allowing me to borrow Mason and Beverly.

 SILHOUETTE BOOKS

ISBN-13: 978-0-373-76753-3
ISBN-10: 0-373-76753-6

FORBIDDEN MERGER

Visit Silhouette Books at www.eHarlequin.com

Printed in U.S.A.

EMILIE ROSE

lives in North Carolina with her college-sweetheart husband and four sons. Writing is Emilie's third (and hopefully her last) career. She's managed a medical office and run a home day care, neither of which offers half as much satisfaction as plotting happy endings. Her hobbies include quilting, gardening and cooking (especially cheesecake). Her favorite TV shows include *ER, CSI* and Discovery Channel's medical programs. Emilie's a country music fan because she can find an entire book in almost any song.

Letters can be mailed to:
Emilie Rose
P.O. Box 20145
Raleigh NC 27619
E-mail: EmilieRoseC@aol.com

THE ELLIOTTS

Patrick m Maeve O'Grady

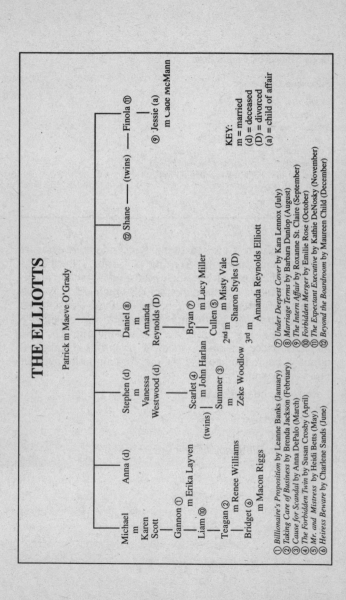

Michael
m
Karen
Scott

Anna (d)

Stephen (d)
m
Vanessa
Westwood (d)

Daniel ⑧
m
Amanda
Reynolds (D)

Shane ⑫ ──── (twins) ──── Finola ⑪

Gannon ①
m Erika Layven

Scarlet ④
m John Harlan

Bryan ⑦
m Lucy Miller

Jessie (a) ⑨
m Cade McMann

Liam ⑩
(twins)

Summer ③
m
Zeke Woodlow

Cullen ⑤
2nd m Misty Vale

Teagan ②
m Renee Williams

Bridget ⑥
m Macon Riggs

3rd m Sharon Styles (D)

Amanda Reynolds Elliott

KEY:
m = married
(d) = deceased
(D) = divorced
(a) = child of affair

① *Billionaire's Proposition* by Leanne Banks (January)
② *Taking Care of Business* by Brenda Jackson (February)
③ *Cause for Scandal* by Anna DePalo (March)
④ *The Forbidden Twin* by Susan Crosby (April)
⑤ *Mr. and Mistress* by Heidi Betts (May)
⑥ *Heiress Beware* by Charlene Sands (June)
⑦ *Under Deepest Cover* by Kara Lennox (July)
⑧ *Marriage Terms* by Barbara Dunlop (August)
⑨ *The Intern Affair* by Roxanne St. Claire (September)
⑩ *Forbidden Merger* by Emilie Rose (October)
⑪ *The Expectant Executive* by Kathie DeNosky (November)
⑫ *Beyond the Boardroom* by Maureen Child (December)

One

Was the guy at the bar checking her out?

No way.

Men who looked like that did not look twice at women who looked like her. Pumps, a pageboy and puny breasts didn't spike testosterone in the average male. Not that he was average. Not by a long shot. But she didn't have time for fun and games.

Aubrey Holt checked her watch. She'd arrived an hour early to scope out the unfamiliar terrain, and she had forty-one minutes remaining before her luncheon´ appointment. That gave her plenty of time to review the questions her father wanted her to ask Liam Elliott, the financial operating officer of Elliott Publication Holdings, the chief rival of Holt Enterprises, her father's company and Aubrey's employer. Something was going on at EPH and no one could figure out what.

Normally, Aubrey would have preferred to meet on familiar turf, but she wanted the F.O.O. of EPH to be comfortable enough to let down his guard and perhaps leak a little insider information. Prying information out of a competitor under the flimsy pretext of an advertiser conflict wasn't Aubrey's preferred method of doing business, but if she wanted to prove her worth to her father, then she'd have to play the game his way. She didn't have to like it, but she'd buckle down and do her best—the way she always did.

As if magnetized, her gaze slid back to the man standing at the bar. He had his back to her and she took advantage of that to shamelessly ogle him, beginning with his polished black wingtips and working her way up the back of his crisply pleated dove-gray trousers to his tush and then over the royal-blue shirt that had to have been custom tailored to fit that narrow waist and those broad shoulders. His dark blond hair was thick and short. Cut by a stylist and not a barber, she'd guess.

And then his gaze trapped hers in the mirror behind the bar. Busted. Her cheeks caught fire. One corner of his mouth lifted and he turned. *Wow.* This man definitely wouldn't need to pick up women in a pub. They probably followed him home in droves.

Blond, Buff And Built lifted his glass in a silent how-about-it toast.

Oh, my God. Aubrey's breath snagged in her windpipe.

At twenty nine, she'd dealt with her share of come-ons. Occasionally, she allowed a gentleman to buy her a drink. But she had *never* looked at a man and wanted to get naked with him before hello. Blue Eyes made her want to get both naked and sweaty. Here. There. Anywhere. The sooner the better. He made her want to act out some of those wild fantasies she only dared think about under the cover of darkness in her lonely apartment.

Too bad she wasn't the type to act out her fantasies. Especially not with a stranger she'd met in a bar.

He headed her way, carving a path easily through the tables and around the waitresses and customers like a skier on a slalom course. Sharp, decisive, athletic. Her heart pounded loudly enough to drown out the patrons of the Irish pub. *Gulp.*

"May I join you?"

Impossible. His voice was as deep as his shoulders were wide. "I'm, um, meeting someone…in a bit."

Darn it.

"Boyfriend?"

"No."

"Then do you mind if I share your table until your friend arrives? The place is packed."

Was it? Aubrey quickly scanned the tables in the long, narrow establishment. All full. And the bar was standing room only. The tables must have filled while she'd been immersed in her list of questions.

Hello! Aubrey Holt, when are you ever going to meet another man like this?

She hastily gathered her papers and shoved them back into her briefcase. "Be my guest. I should have—" she checked her watch "—about thirty-nine minutes left."

Straight white teeth flashed. "About that, huh?"

She concealed a wince. *Could you be more anal, A.?* "Yes."

He hung the suit jacket he'd carried over one arm on the tall coatrack rising from the end of the booth and then slid onto the bench across from her. His knee bumped hers. The light contact hit her like a bolt of lightning, sending electricity storming through her central nervous system like crackling power lines.

She'd guess he was close to six feet. With that body and face he could easily model for fitness magazines. His cologne teased her nose. Cedar? Sandalwood? She couldn't place the brand, which meant nothing except that the manufacturer didn't advertise with any of Holt's magazines.

"You don't come here often." Not a question.

She could drown happily in his Caribbean-blue eyes. "My first time. Do you come here often?"

He nodded. "Best bookmaker's sandwich in New York."

"Bookmaker's?" *Not exactly a brilliant conversationalist today, are you, A.?*

"Ham, pepperoni and Havarti on Irish soda bread with a red-wine vinaigrette that will make your taste buds sing. Or you can try the Guinness Spareribs if you don't mind licking your fingers. They're tender and moist."

And so was she. Listening to the man talk was practically an orgasmic experience. His voice was low enough to make her lean forward to hear him and rough enough to raise the fine hairs on her skin. He had no detectable accent to distinguish where he'd come from. So many Manhattanites hailed from elsewhere. "I'll keep that in mind when I order."

"You do that." He winked.

One dip of those gold-tipped lashes and she considered pulling out her compact to examine her chin for drool. She settled for licking her dry lips. Did she have any lipstick left on? She looked like a lipless lady without. "Do you work nearby?"

"Not close enough that my co-workers will follow me. When I leave the office I like to *leave the office,* if you know what I mean." He grimaced. On him it looked good. But then every expression probably did with a face like that.

"I know exactly what you mean. There are days when I want to run screaming from my office building and never return." She didn't ask his name and didn't offer hers. Fantasy Man had approached her only because he wanted to sit down. After today, she'd probably never see him again.

A totally depressing thought.

"What do you do?" he asked.

Aubrey hesitated. She'd learned the hard way that men saw

her as the yellow brick road to a job with her father's empire, and she'd been burned more than once by mistakenly believing that she was the reason for their interest. "I'm pretty much a Jill-of-all-trades. I do whatever needs doing. You?"

"Number cruncher."

In Manhattan that could mean anything from a Wall Street broker to an accountant, but she couldn't fault him for his vagueness since she hadn't been forthcoming either.

The waitress appeared at the table. "Ready to order?"

Fantasy Man met her gaze. "May I buy you a drink while we wait for our dates?"

She never drank on the job, but what the hell, she'd never tried to weasel information out of a competitor either. The idea left a bitter taste in her mouth and a burn in her stomach. She had approximately thirty-two minutes before that exercise in dishonesty began. "Sure. Thank you. May I have a lemon drop martini?"

The waitress took his order for Woodford Reserve whiskey and departed.

He leaned forward, lacing his fingers on the table. She glanced at his hands. Not manicured, but no ragged nails either. And no wedding ring. How would those hands feel dragging across her skin? *Stop.*

"So, which are you? Sweet or sour?"

The question stumped her. Or was that an estrogen fog making clear thought impossible?

"Sugar on the rim. Sour drink. Sweet and sour. Which are you?" he explained.

Duh. Wake up, Aubrey. "Whichever is required at any given moment. I'm flexible."

A naughty spark flashed in his eyes. "I'll bet you are."

Her entire body flushed hot at the innuendo. "I meant at work."

"So did I." He compressed his lips as if fighting a smile but mischief danced in his eyes.

The fact that she had a business appointment in minutes and there was absolutely no chance of this going too far made her bold enough to return his brazen flirtation. "I'll bet you have amazing stamina. At work."

The corners of his eyes crinkled. "Yeah. I've been known to pull the occasional all-nighter. I'm dedicated to a good outcome. On a project."

Her heart flipped. She'd bet there'd been plenty of female "projects" to keep him occupied. The man oozed sexual confidence but not in the sleazy, slimy, synthetic way of a bar guy trying to pick up women.

The drinks arrived. While he paid the waitress, Aubrey took a healthy sip of her martini. The alcohol hit her empty stomach with a whammy.

"Morning person or night owl?" he asked.

"I like working when the office is empty, so I can be either. I'm flex—" Realizing she'd already said that, she bit off the word.

"Flexible. Yeah. I got that part. You'll have to show me sometime." This time his bright gaze slid from her face to her neck and shoulders and then over the inadequate breasts in her black camisole with its built-in shelf bra. She rarely needed more support. Darn it.

But somehow, she didn't feel flat-chested when he looked at her that way—as if he'd like to see her shed more than the blazer she'd removed when she took the booth in the overheated pub. Her nipples tightened. The flare of his nostrils indicated he'd noticed, and then his gaze returned to hers. Hot. Aroused.

The impact took her breath away and stirred a maelstrom of need low in her belly. She couldn't blame her sudden light-headedness on her drink since she'd only had one sip.

She recalled a scene from a dreadful movie—one in which the lovers had met in the bathroom stall of a crowded restaurant and gone at it like hormonally insane teenagers. Aubrey had snorted in disbelief during the film. Today, the idea not only seemed plausible, it appealed. Even to her. A woman with too many hang-ups, according to her last lover.

She exhaled slowly. Never had she been hit with such a powerful punch of attraction, and she'd certainly never had it reflected back at her with such potency.

Why now, when she couldn't do anything about it, she railed at the unfair Fates.

It's your turn to speak, A. Be witty. Flirt. But when she looked into Fantasy Man's eyes she couldn't think of a thing to say. She was too old and too savvy to be dumbstruck by physical attraction. And yet she was.

He smiled, drawing her attention down his straight nose to the sharply chiseled line of his lips. A small white scar curved on the corner of his not-quite-square jaw. "Like it?"

"What's not to like?" And then she blushed. She *never* blushed and yet he'd made her do so twice in less than five minutes. But he'd caught her gawking. Again.

The crinkles at the corners of his eyes deepened. "The drink. Is it good?"

She wanted to crawl under the table. Of course, if she did he'd probably get the wrong idea about why she was under there, and he'd expect her to get to know him a whole lot better. She should be appalled by the shocking thought. Instead, need tightened in her midsection.

"Oh. Oh, yes. It's delicious. Strong, too." Maybe she could blame her idiocy on the bartender. Aubrey tried to gather her scattered wits before she made an even bigger fool of herself. "So, what about you? Morning person or night owl?"

He shrugged casually, but those twinkling eyes warned her

to brace herself. "Depends on the task. Some things I handle best when I first get up in the morning. Sometimes I do my best work right before I fall into bed."

If her heart beat any harder she'd need a paramedic. He was light years ahead of her in the sexual repartee department. *Aubrey, you have been without a man for too long.* Otherwise his teasing would not make her want to jump him.

"Business or pleasure?" he asked over the rim of his glass.

"Excuse me?"

"Which brings you here today?"

She cursed her slow-functioning brain. "Business. You?"

"Same."

He glanced at his watch. "In fact, my appointment's due any minute."

Wanting to smack her forehead but refraining, she looked beyond his shoulder toward the door. She should have been watching the entrance for her luncheon appointment to arrive. Not that she knew what Liam Elliott looked like, but how many men entered this particular establishment alone at one in the afternoon? Maybe she'd subconsciously blocked her assignation from her mind because she really didn't want to pry information out of the competition. By fair means or foul, her father had ordered.

She checked the time. "Mine, too."

Regret thinned Fantasy Man's mouth. "I see a table opening up. I guess I should take it."

Disappointment settled heavily in her chest. She wasn't ready to let him go. Bantering with him had been fun. When was the last time she'd had fun? She wanted his name and number. *Ask for it.* But somehow she couldn't find the nerve to do so. He was too far out of her league. "Yes, I guess you should. Thanks for the drink and for the company."

"Could I call you?"

Yes! Yes! Yes! she mentally shouted, as pleasure fizzed through her bloodstream like fine champagne, but she replied as calmly as possible, "I'd like that. Very much."

She shuffled through her leather satchel and found a pen but couldn't find anything other than her list of questions to write on. She refused to give him a business card. It would be a while before she'd risk telling him she was a VP for Holt Enterprises, assuming they were still seeing each other in "a while." But writing on a cocktail napkin seemed…cheesy. "I don't have a piece of paper."

He rose, dug into his hanging suit jacket pocket and pulled out a slim gold case. He extracted two business cards, laid both on the table facedown and slid one in her direction. "Write on the back of this. I'll give you my cell and home numbers."

While she wrote her first name and her phone number on the card in front of her he stood beside the booth and penned his numbers on the back of the other. They exchanged cards. He offered his hand, and his fingers closed around hers. His handshake was warm and firm and sent a zing of sexual awareness vibrating though her. From the widening of his pupils and the flare of his nostrils she'd bet the reaction wasn't one-sided.

"It was great meeting you…" Without releasing her hand he looked down at the card and then his gaze, shocked and wary, jerked back to hers. "Aubrey. Aubrey *Holt?*"

How did he know her name? Confused by his reaction, Aubrey flipped the card in her hand and read the embossed letters. Her stomach plunged to her pumps.

"*You're* Liam Elliott?"

"Yes."

She snatched her hand away and cursed her luck. She'd finally met an intelligent man with whom she'd like to pursue a relationship and she not only had to lie to him, but she also had to pry confidential information out of him.

Not the way to win friends or lovers, A.
She fought the urge to scream in frustration.
The sexiest man she'd ever met was totally taboo.

Damn. Double damn, Liam swore silently. Between work difficulties and his mother's battle with breast cancer he hadn't had time to look twice at a woman since January and here he was turned on by the enemy's daughter.

Confusion replaced desire in the most extraordinary violet-colored eyes he'd ever seen. "But you were early."

He stomped on his disappointment. "So were you."

"I…I wanted to familiarize myself with the establishment."

And he'd been driven to drink by this morning's disaster of a meeting between his warring family members—a battle his grandfather had deliberately started nine months ago when he'd announced his pending retirement at the family's New Year's bash. Patrick Elliott's idiotic method for choosing his replacement had pitted his children and grandchildren against each other as they vied for the top spot at EPH.

Worse, Liam suspected his grandfather had used the information Liam had inadvertently shared in devising his plan. Liam was closer to his grandfather than anyone in the family. He and Patrick ate together, golfed together and worked out side by side in the EPH gym. They talked about anything and everything, but Liam now wished he'd kept his mouth shut and had treated his grandfather more like an employer than a relative or a friend. But he'd never expected someone he loved to use his confidences to betray the family.

Why hadn't he seen this coming and found a way to head off disaster? The family counted on him to be the peacemaker. Over the past months Liam had watched his uncles, aunts and cousins become competitors instead of teammates. His grandfather continued to turn a deaf ear to Liam's prediction that the backbiting and squabbling would take EPH down instead of making the company stronger, as Patrick predicted. Liam used to enjoy working in the family business, but the current discord made him dread going to work each day.

He knocked back the last of his drink and considered his options. He could leave, but curiosity kept his feet nailed to the floor. Why had Aubrey Holt called this meeting? Option two: order another drink and join her. But he'd had two in the past hour, breaking his personal code of ethics. He rarely drank during working hours—even though the idea appealed more each day, given the current battlefield where he worked—and he never consumed more than two drinks. Ever. If he did order a third now, he'd probably say to hell with the family, work and ethics and invite Aubrey back to his apartment to see where this attraction would lead—a decision that would cause more trouble than it was worth.

"I— Well." Aubrey visibly switched gears from flirtatious woman to business acquaintance. The spark in her eyes died and determination squared her shoulders and her chin. Her lips firmed, concealing the lush softness.

The thought had crossed Liam's mind that Aubrey might have known who he was when she'd been checking him out at the bar and maybe she'd come on to him to soften him up and worm information out of him, but her obvious horror at discovering his identity erased it.

"Please, have a seat, Mr. Elliott, and let me buy your lunch."

"Liam." Damn, he repeated silently, and slid back into the booth. This time when his knee brushed Aubrey's the fire shooting up his thigh filled him with frustration rather than the heart-racing anticipation he'd felt moments ago. Nothing could come of this attraction. Nothing. Matthew Holt wasn't the kind of adversary to whom you revealed your weaknesses. That meant his daughter wasn't either.

"What made you call my office for an appointment, Aubrey?" He'd be damned if he'd call her Ms. Holt when minutes ago he'd been savoring the idea of getting her out of her clothes and exploring every inch of her long, lean body. With his hands. With his tongue.

He'd been watching her since she walked in. Aubrey might be as tall and slender as a model and not his usual type, but when she'd shimmied out of her black blazer her moves had been worthy of a top-notch stripper. Smooth. Seductive. Riveting. Not that he'd seen any strippers, but he recognized innate sexuality when he saw it.

What's more, he didn't think she'd noticed that he—along with half the other men in Ernie's Pub—had frozen with their glasses halfway to their salivating mouths to watch her wiggle out of that blazer.

She tucked a swath of straight, light brown hair behind her ear. "I, um, wanted to discuss some of our mutual advertisers."

"What about them?"

She shifted on her bench seat and focused on the papers she'd extracted from her briefcase. "There's a rumor that EPH's magazines are deliberately lowering their advertising rates and padding their rate base to lure away Holt's advertisers."

"What? That's nuts. We'd have to falsify our circulation and demographics to do that. We'd lose advertising income and credibility. Besides, you know as well as I do that there are two outside regulatory companies who track those numbers."

With each magazine shooting for maximum profit in his grandfather's contest, there was no way any of the EPH lines would turn away sales dollars. Aubrey's rumor was pure bunk, but it could be damaging if advertisers thought EPH wasn't being truthful.

"Where did you hear that?"

"I, uh, can't reveal my source." Her gaze didn't meet his. She stroked the condensation from her water glass with one finger.

Liam's gaze focused on the slow, gliding digit and sweat, like the droplet on her glass, rolled down his spine. Minutes ago he'd been anticipating her touching him. He severed the unacceptable tangent of his imagination and eyed her suspiciously. Were those seductive moves intentional?

"Has the circulation and advertising fee changed dramatically for some of your magazines over the past year? Are EPH's magazines offering additional marketing services?"

"That's confidential information."

"I know, but the pressure is on for us to stay competitive with the EPH lines."

"What Holt Enterprises does is not my problem."

"I realize that. I was hoping—"

"Hoping I'd give you insider information?" A bitter taste filled his mouth. His grandfather had used Liam's confidences. Was that Aubrey's plan too?

"I was hoping we could work together to get a fair rate from our mutual advertisers and neither company would lose money."

The only thing that kept him from walking out was hunger. That and a prickling at the back of his neck. He never ignored that warning sign. Something wasn't kosher about Aubrey's spiel, but given the stipulations in his grandfather's plan and the disruptions at EPH, it was possible that some of the advertisers had caught wind of the dissention in the Elliott ranks and become unsettled. They'd tried to keep the competition under wraps because Patrick was fanatical about guarding the family name and reputation, but leaks happened.

Liam signaled for the waitress and ordered his regular sandwich. Aubrey ordered the same, but he had the feeling it was more because she didn't want to be bothered with a menu than from any real interest in a bookmaker's special.

"I can't help you. Nothing about the way EPH does business with its advertisers has changed." Nothing except the magazines' personnel were going at each other's throats with fangs bared. His grandfather had decreed that the magazine with the highest profit margin proportionally at the end of the year would see its editor in chief become CEO of EPH. Nobody wanted to lose.

As financial operating officer Liam was in charge of tracking the numbers. The weight rested heavily on his shoulders. He'd had to take his personal feelings out of the equation, forget the people involved and deal strictly with the cold, hard facts. It wasn't easy. He worried about EPH and worried about his mother even more.

And while his extended family self-destructed around him Liam realized life was passing him by. He was thirty-one. His parents had been married and had four children by his age. Even his brothers and sister had wised up. Gannon had married in February. He and his wife Erika were expecting their first child. Liam's younger brother Tag was engaged, and his sister Bridget had recently married a Colorado sheriff and left the family business. He also had a handful of cousins and an uncle who'd recently found their significant others.

All Liam had was a long history of hooking up with the wrong women, a job in the family business, a Porsche he rarely drove—but shelled out a fortune for in parking fees— and a Park Avenue apartment he only used for sleeping. He had no one to stand by and support him the way his father had supported Liam's mother through her ordeal.

His workaholic father had risen several notches in Liam's

opinion over the past nine months by getting his priorities straight. Family first. Work second. It hadn't always been that way. It had taken almost losing his wife to set Michael Elliott straight.

The sandwiches arrived and the server departed.

Aubrey's violet eyes met Liam's and the impact hit him like a fist in the gut, knocking the breath out of him. "How is your mother? I read about her illness in the paper."

What was she—psychic? "She's improving. She's finished chemotherapy and her hair's growing back."

"Her diagnosis must have been terrifying for all of you."

"Yes." He could have lost his mother, and while she wasn't out of the woods yet and wouldn't be until she'd been cancer-free for five years, optimism was on the upswing. The doctors gave her a good prognosis.

"You're close to her?"

"Now more than ever. Are you close to your mother?"

Sadness filled Aubrey's eyes. "No. She left my father when I was eleven. She couldn't stand always coming in second to Dad's mistress—work."

"You didn't keep in touch?"

"I shuffled back and forth for a while, but then she remarried." Aubrey ducked her head and the curtain of her shiny hair swung forward. "The sandwich is good and you're right about the vinaigrette. It's delicious."

He ignored her bid to switch topics. "You didn't get along with the new husband?"

Color leeched from Aubrey's face. "He liked me a little too much."

The sandwich turned to rubber in Liam's mouth. "He came on to you?"

Aubrey abandoned her lunch. "Yes."

Anger percolated in Liam's veins. "How old were you?"

"Sixteen."

"Did your mother divorce the bastard?"

"No. Look, could we talk about something else?"

His appetite deserted him. He wanted to ask how her mother could stay with the pervert and if her father had beaten the crap out of him. But he didn't. "Sure."

"I heard Patrick is considering retirement. Any idea who will replace him?"

Liam rested his fists beside his plate. "Aubrey, I'm not going to discuss EPH."

She abandoned the pretzel she'd been nibbling. "I understand. I'm sorry I wasted your time."

He didn't understand the emotions chasing across her face. Disappointment was easy to identify, but he'd swear he saw failure in Aubrey Holt's eyes. Why? "You haven't. Until you started with the EPH interrogation I was having the best time I've had in months."

Her lips parted and color washed her cheeks. Before she could reply his cell phone rang. He unclipped it from his belt. "Excuse me. Liam Elliott."

"Mr. Elliott, this is Trisha at the Davenport Gallery. Gilda Raines has agreed to talk about parting with the painting you wanted for your mother. I'd suggest you come now. Gilda is…unique. She wants to meet you before she makes her decision."

"I'll be right there." He snapped the phone shut and signaled for the waitress. "I hate to cut this short, but I have to go."

"Problem at work?"

A wry smile tugged his lips. Did Aubrey never give up? "No. I've been trying for months to buy a painting by my mother's favorite artist. The artist has finally agreed to discuss selling. I don't want to give her time to change her mind. I'm going to meet her now."

"Which artist?"

He reached for his wallet. "Gilda Raines."

Aubrey sat up, alert and radiating excitement. "Are you serious? She's my favorite, too. And you're going to meet her! She's a recluse who never meets *anyone*." Her hand covered his on the table and sparks hopped up his arm. "May I come with you?"

Liam looked across the table at the enemy's daughter, at her pale, slender hand over his. A wise man would cut his losses and say goodbye. *Now.* Evidently he wasn't as smart as he thought he was because the shine in those violet eyes and the curve of her lips overrode his conscience's objections.

"You can ride along. But I'm not answering questions about EPH. If you ask even one I'll have the cab pull over and put you out. Are we clear?"

Her grin stole his breath. "As clear as the Hope Diamond."

Two

Aubrey wanted to get to know Liam better, but putting her hand in his lap wasn't quite what she had in mind. She hadn't hit ground zero, but she'd come close enough that he inhaled sharply and his warm thigh muscles tensed beneath her fingers.

"Sorry." She snatched her hand away and dug her nails into the armrest on the car door, bracing herself as the taxi zig-zagged around slower cars.

"Not a problem." His voice sounded tight.

Her palm continued to tingle long after it left Liam's rock-hard thigh behind, all the way down Lexington Avenue, in fact. Awareness whizzed through her veins. The cabbie drove like a carjacker evading the law, but that wasn't surprising considering Liam had offered to double his fare if he'd get them to the gallery fast.

Another swerve pitched her back against the hard-mus-cled, good-smelling, taboo man beside her. Their shoulders bumped and their eyes met. Liam's gaze slowly lowered to her mouth. Aubrey's breath caught and her heart raced.

How would he kiss? Soft or hard? Reserved or passionate? She'd never know. She turned to look back out the window and a disappointed sigh slipped past her lips.

The cab pulled to the curb in front of the gallery. Aubrey said a silent prayer of thanks and climbed out while Liam paid the fare.

He joined her on the sidewalk. "You said you like this artist?"

"Yes. Her paintings are very sensual."

"They're flowers," he said with a straight face.

Aubrey studied the confused frown on Liam's face. Did he not know anything about the artist? "Have you ever studied Georgia O'Keeffe?"

He shook his head. "Only enough to know vaguely who she is. Art's not my thing."

What were his interests outside of work? She'd never know that either. Disappointment weighed heavily on her shoulders.

"Gilda Raines has been compared to a modern-day O'Keeffe although she's more likely to paint the flowers and scenes from the Southeast rather than the Southwest. She's originally from Charleston, South Carolina, and she took up painting after her husband, the love of her life, died. I've heard she's quite an unusual personality."

She followed him inside a bright, open area. Oils of varying sizes graced the walls and a few pieces of sculpture stood on wide pedestals scattered throughout the space.

A chic brunette approached. "Mr. Elliott?"

"Yes."

"Trisha Evans." In Aubrey's estimation, the handshake lasted longer than it should have. "And you are?"

"Aubrey Holt."

"Ms. Raines is waiting for you in the private viewing room.

Follow me." She turned and led the way. Aubrey wondered if the woman normally sashayed that way or if she'd widened the pendulum swing of her hips for Liam's benefit. And then Aubrey rolled her eyes. What did it matter if the woman wanted to advertise her wares? Aubrey would probably be doing the same thing if Liam's last name were anything but Elliott.

A woman no more than five feet tall awaited them. Her face held remarkably few lines for someone in her late sixties. The morning glory painting on the easel beside her took Aubrey's breath away. It wasn't one she had seen before. This painting seemed to express everything she'd felt before she'd discovered Liam's identity.

"So you wanna buy my painting," Gilda Raines said without preamble in a rich southern drawl, drawing Aubrey's attention momentarily away from the mesmerizing artwork. The artist's dark eyes assessed Liam.

"Yes, ma'am." He briefly glanced at the framed oil.

Ms. Evans barely finished with the introductions before Ms. Gaines asked, "Why?"

"I explained about my mother in my letter. About her illness."

Aubrey's gaze jerked to Liam. He'd written to the artist?

"I don't get many letters begging me to sell—especially a painting someone has never seen. Anything, you said. 'I'll buy anything.' I don't part with my babies often, Mr. Elliott, and when I do it's for a good reason. I don't know that I should give up one now. Why should I?"

"Because my mother admires your work and having one of your paintings will make her happy."

Thin arms crossed over a loose-fitting paisley print shirt. Gilda remained mute, but her expression said, "Not good enough."

Even though it wasn't any of her business, Aubrey butted

in. "Because after a double mastectomy his mother needs to be reminded she's a woman."

All three heads swiveled toward Aubrey. "Your morning glory embodies womanhood, femininity and sexuality. I'm guessing Karen Elliott feels she's lacking all of those qualities at the moment."

Gaines's eyes narrowed and she cocked her head. "How would you know?"

Memories encroached, robbing a little of the brightness from Aubrey's afternoon. "I lost a friend to breast cancer last year. I spent time with her during her treatment. Quite a few of your paintings hang in the Women's Health Center. *The Daylily* is my favorite, but Jane liked *The Gardenia* best."

Jane, her father's personal assistant for as far back as Aubrey could remember, had lost her life to the disease after a long, valiant struggle. The heartbreaking shame of it was that if Jane had gone for the mammograms her doctor had been recommending for the past two decades they might have caught the cancer in time to save her life, but Jane had been afraid the procedure would be uncomfortable and embarrassing so she'd put it off only to learn too late that the hell of chemotherapy was much worse than the slight discomfort of a mammogram.

Grief reopened in Aubrey's chest. She pressed a hand over her aching heart and turned back to the artwork to blink away her tears. For as far back as she could remember she'd talked more to Jane than to her socialite mother or workaholic father, and Aubrey still missed Jane, her confidante and hero.

It had been Jane who'd realized something was wrong after Aubrey's mother had remarried and Jane who'd pried the confession out of Aubrey about her stepfather's inappropriate advances. And it had been Jane who'd gone to her boss and revealed the sordid truth. Aubrey had been swiftly removed from her mother's home and she hadn't been allowed to visit again. When her mother wanted to see her she'd had to come to the Holt apartment. She hadn't come often.

Gilda joined Aubrey beside the painting and tipped her head to indicate Liam. "Do you think he gets it?"

Aubrey blinked away the past and looked over her shoulder at Liam. The careful neutrality of his face confirmed he didn't understand the nuances behind the flower. And then she met Gilda's skeptical gaze. "I can explain it to him."

Gilda cackled and nodded. "Yes, I'm sure you can. All right, then."

And just that quickly the deal was done. Minutes later the artwork had been packaged and placed in the trunk of a taxi and Aubrey and Liam were on the way to Liam's apartment—a decision Aubrey considered both wise and foolhardy. Wise because she might be able to glean more information from Liam, but also foolhardy because she was only tormenting herself with what she couldn't have.

The cabbie drove as aggressively as the first even without the added incentive of a double fare. He swerved to avoid a bicycle messenger at the last possible second, pitching Aubrey practically into Liam's lap. Liam's strong hands steadied her.

She lifted her gaze to his. "Excuse me."

The blue of his eyes darkened and his gaze dropped to her lips. "No problem."

Aubrey ordered her muscles to move her away from the warmth and strength of Liam's grasp. They mutinied. Liam's hand lifted from her upper arm to cup her jaw. He stroked her cheekbone with his thumb and then threaded his fingers through her hair. Aubrey shivered and inhaled a shaky breath.

Why oh why did this man have to be the one to awaken every feminine instinct in her body?

Before she could force herself to retreat, Liam's head lowered. Instead of scooting back to her side of the slippery vinyl seat Aubrey lifted her chin and met him halfway.

His lips brushed hers, softly at first and then more insistently. Her pulse raced. Her lungs seized. And then his slick tongue parted her lips and she tasted him. Delicious. Aubrey covered his hand on her face, determined to remove it, but somehow her fingers threaded through his and her other hand clenched the lapel of his jacket.

The movement of the car rocked her breast against his bicep, stroking with each swerve and bump in the road and causing her nipples to tighten and warmth to puddle low in her belly. And then Liam's arms banded around her and he lifted her across the seat and into his lap. She gasped at the suddenness of the action, at the heat of his thighs beneath hers and his groin against her hip.

A second of sanity prevailed, and she drew back to gasp for breath, but she didn't go far. Her forehead rested on his. Their noses touched. His heart slammed beneath her palm and his breath swept her skin.

"What are we doing?" she whispered.

"Damned if I know." One of his hands raked up and down her spine. The other settled on her hip and stroked downward until he found skin. The hem of her knee-length skirt had ridden up to midthigh. She wasn't wearing stockings. His hot palm glided over her knee, down her calf and back up again, edging beneath the fabric.

This really had to stop…in a minute. Aubrey couldn't remember ever being so aroused so quickly and in such an inappropriate location—a cab, for pity's sake, in plain view of the driver up front. Liam kissed one corner of her mouth and then the other, and then he took her bottom lip into his teeth and gently tugged. His tongue laved the sensitive inner skin.

A sound, half-moan, half-whimper, bubbled in her throat. She struggled for lucidity. "This is not… I didn't… I wasn't looking for this today."

Liam's chest rose and fell on a deep breath. "I know."

"We shouldn't. You're the competition."

The hand on her thigh tightened before grazing upward over her hip, beneath her blazer and past her waist to rest just below her breast. "I know that, too."

Don't stop. Dizziness forced Aubrey to suck in a forgotten breath. One more kiss, she promised herself as she arched against him. Just one. She angled her head and took his mouth, savoring the taste of forbidden fruit. His thumbnail scraped over her nipple and a moan poured from her mouth into his. She twined her tongue around the slickness of his and then suckled. His chest vibrated beneath her palm in a purely masculine purr, and he shifted on the seat, pulling her closer and bringing the hot shaft of his erection flush against her hip. Heat flooded her core and moisture dampened her skin. She tingled all over as if she'd been dunked in a warm champagne bath.

"We're here, bud," the taxi driver's heavy Bronx accent interrupted. Liam's muscles turned rigid beneath her.

Shocked by her uncharacteristically brazen behavior, Aubrey scrambled out of Liam's lap and back to her side of the cab. Her face—her entire body—burned. Rather than look at Liam, she glanced out the car window and blinked in surprise. Park Avenue? Liam lived only a few blocks away from her place on Fifth. Walking distance. Her heart missed a beat. So close…and yet worlds apart because of their employers.

Liam opened the door and offered his hand. Wisdom decreed Aubrey say goodbye and give the driver her address. But she'd promised Gilda Raines that she'd explain the painting to Liam.

You don't have to. His mother will understand it and Gilda will never know.

But you promised.

And she didn't break promises.

Snatching up her purse and her leather satchel, she slid across the seat, placed her hand in Liam's and let him help her from the car. She quickly released his hold when a fresh wave of longing swept through her.

This can't happen. But her mind and body didn't seem to be speaking the same language. Turning away from temptation, she studied the gray stone building and waited on the sidewalk while the cabbie removed the painting from the trunk.

A doorman rushed from the apartment building. "Need help with that, Mr. Elliott?"

"No thanks, Carlos, I have it."

Aubrey followed the men into the building and across the marble floor past a bank of elevators to a private elevator located at the end of a short hall. Private elevators meant one thing. Penthouse. She'd had fantasies about elevators, a handsome stranger and a blackout. She'd never even considered having an elevator all to herself and not having to rely on being trapped by a power outage to pursue her naughty dream. She shouldn't be thinking that now, but knowing the man had the power to lower her IQ fifty points with a single kiss and that he had his own elevator sent her mind sprinting down a dangerous alley.

Everyone in Manhattan or magazine publishing knew the Elliotts were wealthy, but she'd had no idea Liam owned such an expensive piece of real estate. Or maybe he didn't. Maybe like her he rented a family-owned property. Aubrey loved her bright and airy apartment, but she sometimes wished for more independence. She and her father had an odd relationship. Aubrey yearned for his approval, but she wished she didn't. Being on her own… She sighed. Probably wouldn't change a thing. Her father would continue to give her everything she wanted materially, but nothing emotionally.

The elevator doors closed, leaving the doorman behind. Aubrey faced forward, but turning her back on Liam didn't help. Dark wood wainscoting covered the bottom half of the doors and walls of the elevator, but the top half was mirrored. No matter which way she looked she faced multiples of Liam's reflection. He surrounded her. She lowered her gaze to the marble floor.

"You get used to it," he said, drawing her eyes back to his. "The mirrors," he added when she lifted an eyebrow.

He rested the painting on the floor and shoved his free hand in his pocket. His relaxed pose would have fooled her if not for the intensity in the blue eyes watching her. She didn't know what to say. Evidently, her adolescent, tongue-tied stupor had returned.

The doors glided open into a small carpeted hall containing two doors, one on the left and another on the right. So the elevator wasn't exclusively Liam's. It would take a power outage to ensure privacy, after all—not that it mattered since she and Liam wouldn't be doing the deed in the elevator or anywhere else.

He unlocked the door on the right and motioned for her to precede him. Aubrey walked through the dark wooden portal. Her heels tapped across the granite floor leading into Liam's living room. The warm wood tones, scatter rugs and traditional furniture and fabrics surprised her. She'd expected a bachelor pad to look more like…well, a bachelor pad. Black leather, chrome, fur rugs. But other than the granite floor, his home had none of those I-am-man-hear-me-roar attributes. Jewel tones of emerald, ruby and sapphire dominated a decor that was surprisingly classic and very similar to her tastes. A couple of landscapes hung on the walls. Vineyards, unless she missed her guess.

The man continued to surprise her. Too bad she couldn't hang around to uncover the rest of his secrets.

"Tell me why three women just looked at me like I was a pitiful dumbass." Liam balanced the heavy frame across the arms of a wing chair.

Aubrey's grin hit him in the solar plexus. "Didn't like that, did you? Here let me do that."

She approached to help him remove the paper from the painting. Their fingers tangled as they reached for the same piece of tape. It was a wonder the sparks between them didn't ignite the heavy brown paper protecting the artwork. Liam jerked too hard and a tearing sound rent the air.

"Careful," she said. "You're going to want to rewrap this to take it to your mother." She carefully removed the remainder of the paper and then placed it on the floor beside the chair. Stepping back, she tilted her head and observed the picture. "Tell me what you see."

Liam looked at the painting. "A white flower with a magenta center surrounded by green vines."

Aubrey closed the distance between them. Her shoulder brushed his. In her heels she stood almost eye to eye with him. "Focus on the vines. What do you see?"

Violet eyes. Sleek, milk-chocolate hair. Smooth ivory skin. Her scent filled his senses. Roses? Gardenias? Something floral and heady, reminiscent of hot summer evenings at The Tides, his grandparents' estate in the Hamptons. If the kiss they'd shared in the taxi had shaken Aubrey as much as it had him she didn't show it.

Sunlight streamed through the window, heating his skin.

He shrugged out of his suit coat and tossed it over the back of the sofa and then transferred his attention from the woman who had his hormones in an uproar to the piece in question. "Curves. The vines are curvy."

"Resemble anything you've seen before?"

"Yes. Plants." His tone and expression must have revealed his frustration.

She reached out and traced a fingertip over the thickest vine. "Look again."

He felt stupid—neither a familiar nor welcome feeling. "Hills. Valleys…" And then it clicked, and it was so obvious he didn't know how he'd missed the shape before. "A woman's body. Reclining."

Each leaf and vine shimmered like wrinkled emerald-green satin sheets and the woman's form lay right in the middle. Damn, how had he missed that?

Because any man who wasn't thinking about sex would only see a tangle of vines.

"Very good." Her approving smile filled him with an inordinate amount of warmth. "Now look at the morning glory itself. Notice the dew trembling on the edge of the blossom and the curling tendrils of the shoots surrounding the flower."

Her description made it impossible for him to miss the hidden meaning. Liam's ears burned and he swore. "I bought a pornographic painting for my mother."

Aubrey's low chuckle danced down his spine. "No, you bought her a sensual one. There's nothing dirty about this picture."

"If that symbolizes what I think it does, then I can't give it to her."

"Gilda Raines paints of life, birth, femininity and sensuality. Like you said, it's just a flower to the uninformed observer, but to someone who looks deeper it's the cradle of life."

"It's a woman's—"

She held up a hand to stop him. "Liam, don't make this ugly. It's a beautiful piece. Your mother will adore it."

She turned back to the painting. The way Aubrey looked at it—with parted lips and flushed cheeks—was the same way she'd looked at him before they'd exchanged names and again right before he'd kissed her. The air in the room thickened. He shoved his hands through his hair. He should call her a cab before sexual attraction and thoughts of this…*erotic* picture overrode his good sense.

His brain and his mouth took opposite paths. "Can I take your jacket and get you a glass of wine?"

She hesitated, catching her bottom lip between her teeth. Her gaze traveled to the door and back to him as if she, too, were weighing the wisdom of staying. "Yes."

Politeness demanded he step forward and help her remove her blazer, but watching her shimmy out of the black garment impeded the blood flow to his cerebral cortex. Mesmerized, he watched one bare shoulder appear and then the other. Her camisole top with its pencil-thin straps clung lovingly to her slender figure.

He'd noticed her sensuality at the pub. Her interpretation of the painting confirmed it. Aubrey Holt was undoubtedly the sexiest woman Liam had ever encountered. He'd never experienced such strong magnetism in his life. Who she was didn't dampen his response in the slightest.

Desire pulsed heavily in his groin and tightened his rib cage, making it impossible to draw a deep breath. She extended her arm with the jacket in her hand. Liam took it. Without turning he pitched the garment in the direction of the sofa, curled his fingers around her waist and pulled her forward until her body pressed flush against his. Aubrey's breath hitched a second before his mouth covered hers.

Her lips parted immediately, welcoming and meeting the thrust of his tongue. She tasted better than the finest wine in his collection. Her arms wound around his neck, pulling him closer, pressing her breasts against his chest.

He usually dated petite women, usually had to bend himself in half for a kiss, but Aubrey rose on her tiptoes and their bodies aligned perfectly. Breast to chest. Thigh to thigh. Her feminine mound cradled his erection and when she arched her back and ground against him, electricity crackled down to his toes, up to his skull and back again to settle hot and heavy below his belt. He cupped her tight buttocks and pushed back, relishing the way her whimper filled his lungs.

Skin. He needed skin. He raked his hands upward, dragging the hem of her top from her skirt, and then he found the warm satin of her waist and the ridge of her spine with his fingertips. She shivered in his arms and drew back to gasp. He dipped his head, burying his face in the juncture of her neck and shoulder, tasting her sweetness, inhaling her heady fragrance, feeling her rapid pulse against his tongue. His heart hammered as if he'd raced up the stairs to the twenty-fifth floor of the EPH building. His lungs burned. And he ached to lose himself in the dewy center of the woman in his arms.

Desire. That's it. That's what the painting represented. A woman on the brink of desire.

A single brain cell broke through the surface of the testosterone flooding him. This was Aubrey. Aubrey *Holt.* The enemy's daughter. Liam drew back, breathing heavily, and looked into Aubrey's passion-darkened eyes. This wasn't love. It was pure, unadulterated lust. He'd experienced lust before, but never like this, never this potent, never this intoxicating. "Aubrey?"

He hoped like hell she had the strength to end this, because he didn't think he did. Her damp lips quivered. She blinked as if trying to clear the haze from her heavy-lidded, dark-lashed eyes, and then she lowered her gaze and her hands to his waist. But instead of pushing him away, she yanked his shirttails from his pants.

Liam sucked in a sharp breath. Every muscle in his body clenched rock hard as she bared his chest one button at a time. When she spread her palms and swept them over his skin, he shuddered and then quickly lifted his arms above his head to unfasten his cuff links. He pitched them onto the end table with a clatter and then his shirt hit the floor. Her fingers fumbled with his belt and he nearly lost it.

Catching her wrists, he stilled her hands and then released her and reached for her top. He whisked it over her head and groaned at what he discovered. No bra. Dark puckered tips crested her small breasts, and his mouth watered in anticipation of tasting her. She lifted her hands as if to cover herself, but he beat her to it, covering her warm flesh. Her nipples prodded his palms. He caressed her in a circular motion and the taut tips beaded even harder. Each circle coiled something achy and tight deep inside him.

Aubrey's head fell back on a moan. Her fingers tangled in his hair and she tugged. Liam didn't refuse the invitation. He bent, stroked his tongue over her sensitive tip, raked her gently with his teeth and then suckled deeply. Her nails dug into his shoulders. He transferred his attention to the opposite breast and rubbed slick fingers over the one he'd abandoned.

Her knees buckled. Liam caught her up in his arms and carried her to his bedroom. One, because he wanted to savor every inch of her. Two, because he needed condoms. He'd long since outgrown the need to carry them in his wallet. His affairs these days, though few and far between, were planned like dessert after dinner. He never had lunch and an unexpected afternoon delight. Maybe the surprise factor explained why Aubrey had hit him so hard.

The love bite she planted on his neck derailed his train of thought. He almost walked into a wall. Her teeth teased his earlobe seconds before her tongue traced his ear. Embers ignited in his gut. He quickened his stride, reached his bedroom and set her on her feet beside his bed. He hadn't bothered to open the drapes this morning, but a sliver of afternoon sunlight seeped through the gap between them, slashing across his bed like a laser pointer indicating, "Here. Now."

No kidding. The ray of light was much easier to understand than a painting about female body parts.

Liam sat down on the micro suede comforter and turned Aubrey around so that her back faced him. He strung a line of openmouthed kissed along her vertebrae while his suddenly clumsy fingers fumbled to release the back button and zip of her pencil skirt. The skirt crumpled to the floor. He vaguely registered her kicking it and her shoes aside, but his gaze was fastened on her bottom in—heaven help him—a thong and nothing else. Black. Satiny. Tiny. He traced the waistband and then the strip between her cheeks. Goose bumps rose on her pale skin. His blood rushed south, leaving him dizzy with desire and gasping for breath. Impatient, he hooked the black bands with his thumbs and pushed them down her legs.

She stepped out and turned. Like a kid with a giant ice-cream sundae, Liam could only stare, not knowing where to start or which flavor to sample first. His hands found her breasts. His mouth skimmed her belly, edging downward in sips and nips toward her tangled brown curls. She trembled. The tiny quakes traveled up his arms, through his lips. He lifted his head and met her slumberous gaze.

"Please," she whispered. "I need to touch you, too."

An offer too good to refuse. Liam rose.

Aubrey tackled his belt and then the hook of his slacks. Her knuckles dragged across his erection as she lowered his zipper, and stars exploded behind his tightly closed lids. She shoved his pants and briefs down his thighs. He distracted himself from her mind-numbing caresses by mapping her slight curves with his hands, learning her body the way a blind man reads Braille, by feel. He found the crisp curls and delved into the slick moisture they concealed.

Her gasped "Yes" encouraged him to stroke long and slow until he discovered her magic spot, and then he teased her with short, quick brushes over the swollen flesh before dipping deeper. She arched into his touch, pressed hungry kisses along his jaw, until he covered her mouth with his and mimicked the thrust of his fingers with his tongue.

She clung to his shoulders as release shuddered through her. Her cries filled his mouth and then she collapsed against him, skin to skin. Liam slowly eased his fingers from her dampness and ripped back the bedding. When he turned around again, Aubrey was on her knees in front of him, her passion-glazed eyes gazing up at him.

He ground his molars, clenched his fists and prayed she'd give him a second to recover before she touched him. If she didn't, his afternoon delight would be over in a nanosecond. He didn't have a snowball's chance in hell of lasting if she put her mouth on him.

Three

At the pub Aubrey had tagged Liam as buff, blond and built. The description didn't begin to do justice to the man in front of her. Liam hadn't developed those thick muscles sitting behind a desk. He worked out.

Aubrey skated her palms up his hair-roughened calves and thighs. His long, thick erection jerked as she brushed past the tangle of wiry dark blond curls to shove on his hips so he'd sit down. Liam sat, knees splayed but cuffed by his pants at his ankles. Aubrey debated leaning in for a taste of him, but the urgency pulsing through her veins insisted she hurry rather than linger. Judging by the taut tendons of Liam's neck, she knew he teetered just as close to the edge of control as she.

She quickly removed his shoes, socks and pants and tossed them aside. Bracing her hands on his thighs, she levered herself to stand before him. The desire in his eyes poured over her like heated oil, burning, but in a good way. An incredibly arousing, blood-boiling way. Not something she'd previously experienced.

He lifted her hands, sketched a nerve-tingling erotic kiss in each palm with his tongue and then transferred her hands to his shoulders. His satiny skin stretched tight over corded muscle. She couldn't resist tracing each swell and crevice, and raking her fingers through the coils of burnished gold spattering his chest.

Liam's hot mouth found one breast. His talented fingers teased the other. When he devoured her that way, stroked and molded her that way, Aubrey didn't feel inadequate, unwomanly. Despite the breathtaking release he'd just given her, her body tightened once again, hungry for more. "Please, Liam. I can't wait."

He lifted his head, his gaze locking with hers, and then he reached for the bedside table, opened the drawer and extracted a square packet.

Condoms. She'd forgotten. So unlike her. But then everything about today was beyond her realm. She'd never fallen in instant lust, never become intimate with a near stranger.

He slowly rose, sliding inch by inch of his hot skin against hers. For heart-stopping seconds his shaft burned against her navel and then he leaned back and ripped the packet open with his teeth.

Aubrey stroked his back, his waist, his firm buttocks, bringing her hands around to curl her fingers around his thickness and cup the heaviness below. Her thumb found a slick droplet and smoothed it over his silky skin.

His breath whistled through clenched teeth. He muttered a curse and ground out, "Enough."

He brushed her hands aside, donned protection and urged her onto the bed. With one foot still on the floor, Aubrey leaned back across the oyster-colored sheets and lifted a hand, beckoning him into her arms. The mattress dipped under his weight. His hands, hot and slightly rough, cupped her bottom and lifted as he stood beside the bed and positioned himself. Aubrey's breath caught in anticipation and then gushed from her lungs as he plunged deeply, filling her with a solid thrust.

He withdrew and thrust again and again. She arched to meet him and then reached up and curled her fingers around his nape to pull him closer. Liam planted his hands beside her head. His molten blue gaze locked with hers and his biceps bulged as he slowly lowered until his chest hairs teased her breasts. His breath stirred the fine hairs on her neck and then finally, *finally,* his lips sealed hers. She hooked one leg around his hips, drawing him back each time he withdrew and urging him to go faster and deeper as everything inside her twisted tighter and she raced toward another climax.

Ecstasy hit hard and fast, rocking her and robbing her breath. She threw her head back and cried out as Liam slammed into her and groaned as his own orgasm undulated over him.

Breathing heavily, he collapsed to his elbows and buried his face beside hers on the bed. Aubrey traced the line of his spine and he shivered against her. The weight of him, the heat of him, blanketed her in a sensual cocoon. A satisfied smile curved her lips and a sense of well-being flooded her, weighting her limbs and her eyelids. Bliss.

Her racing heart and laboring lungs slowed and then with a sudden icy shower her conscience washed away the haze of desire.

What had she done?

She'd taken the enemy to bed and in doing so guaranteed she'd disappoint her father yet again, because she couldn't sleep with Liam and then betray him.

* * *

Aubrey stiffened beneath Liam and then shoved hard against his shoulders. He forced his drained and satiated muscles into action and rolled to her side, reluctantly disengaging from the slick heat of her body.

She pressed her fingers to the pleat between her eyebrows. Regret tightened her features and flattened her luscious, kiss-swollen mouth.

Liam's stomach clenched as reality sank in.

"That shouldn't have happened," Aubrey whispered as she reached for the sheet, dragging it across her body and sliding to the edge of the bed.

"Probably not." No probably about it. This afternoon had been a mistake. They both knew it. Chalk it up to his unerring ability to choose the wrong woman.

"I have to go." She clutched the sheet with one hand and reached for her skirt with the other. The bed sheet tethered her inches short of her goal, and she didn't look like she wanted to release it and let him see her naked. Ridiculous, considering the taste of her still lingered on his lips.

He scooped up her skirt, passed it to her and then raked a hand through his hair. "Aubrey—"

Without looking at him, she held up a hand like a traffic cop. "Please. No post mortems."

What could he say? There could be no future in any relationship between them. And for the first time in Liam's life that bothered him. Until now he'd been the king of dead-end-and-damned-happy-about-it relationships.

He rolled his tense shoulders. Blame it on all the new shiny jewelry being shoved in his face at EPH. Wedding and engagement rings had multiplied like bacteria among the staff—Elliotts in particular. His grandfather's aim might have been to increase productivity with his little competition, but what he'd done was run off employees and cause a rash of romances.

"Would you like to shower first or—"

"No. No, I need to go." She shimmied her skirt over her long, lean legs and her round, tight, bare butt. Watching her move made his pulse accelerate and his groin tighten all over again.

"Can I call you a cab?"

With her arms crossed over her chest, she shoved her feet into her shoes and bolted out the bedroom door. "No. Thank you."

He yanked on his pants, ducked into the bathroom to ditch the condom and followed her into the den. She dragged on her top, shrugged on her jacket, snatched up her purse and briefcase and wasted no time hustling toward the door. She still hadn't looked at him. That stung.

"Aubrey, wait." He planted a palm on the door, holding it closed.

She paused with her hand on the knob. Her spine remained steel-girder stiff, and she kept her chin tucked as if she wanted to hide from what had just happened.

Well, didn't that make him feel like a damned prize?

Her scent, a heady floral mingled with hot sex, filled Liam's lungs as he inhaled. He battled the unaccustomed urge to smooth her tangled hair and straighten the tucked-under collar of her blazer. "We used protection and I'm clean, but if you need anything you have my numbers."

She turned and met his gaze. Panic and regret darkened her eyes. "I won't call, Liam. I can't."

"Yeah. I guess you're right. My family's in enough turmoil without throwing an affair with the enemy's daughter into the pot."

Her mouth dropped open and a wounded expression

briefly crossed her face before she blinked it away. "The enemy? That's how you see my father?"

He cursed his clumsy tongue. "Matthew Holt and my grandfather have had a few run-ins. Holt Enterprises and EPH don't always see eye to eye on how we conduct business."

"No. No, they don't. You're right. I hope your mother likes the painting. Goodbye, Liam." She yanked open his door and then quietly closed it behind her.

Liam banged his forehead against the wood and then slowly turned to face the painting. Where was his brain? The afternoon shouldn't have happened. He should have left the pub the minute Aubrey started with her prying questions. He shouldn't have taken her to the gallery or brought her home for a lesson in Art 101. He sure as hell shouldn't have taken her to bed. Because today he'd had the best sex of his life and there was absolutely no chance that he'd ever repeat the experience.

He cursed all the way back to his bedroom. Aubrey's scent clung to his skin and to his bed. Determined to remove all traces of her from his apartment, he ripped off the sheets. As he shoved them into the hamper for his housekeeper to wash, he caught sight of his watch.

Damn. He hadn't called work to tell them he wouldn't be returning after his luncheon appointment. A first. He never missed work. Hell, for the past nine months he'd practically lived in the EPH building. He headed for the phone on his bedside table. A sliver of black sticking out from under his bed stopped him in his tracks. He bent and scooped it up. Aubrey's thong. His pulse rate tripled. He should return it. But how?

Mail? Nah, he didn't think so.

In person? Hell, no. That would be stepping right back into the fire. He couldn't risk his family—particularly his grandfather, who believed appearances were everything—finding out about today.

For several seconds he studied the black satin dangling from his fingers and then he crushed the lingerie in his hand and shoved it in his nightstand drawer.

He couldn't have Aubrey, but he could have the memories of this wild afternoon to fuel his fantasies when the only lover he had was his right hand.

"Happy to have you home again, Mom. I brought a bottle of champagne to celebrate." Liam set the champagne on the coffee table and bent over the chaise in the den of the family brownstone to kiss his mother's cheek.

She had a little more color in her face than she'd had when he'd visited her at The Tides a couple of weeks ago, and she'd lost some of the gauntness hollowing her cheeks. Short tufts of newly grown hair, more gray than before, peeked from the scarf she wore over her head.

Liam nodded hello to his father. He and his father had never been close. Michael Elliott had spent too much of Liam's childhood at work, leaving Liam to rely on his grandfather for mentorship as the years passed.

"You and your wine collection. Thank you." Karen Elliott shifted her legs to the side and patted the cushion. "Sit down, Liam. It's good to be home. Your grandparents' estate is a wonderful place to recuperate, but it's time for me to get on with life. Besides, you've all spent way too much time worrying about me and traipsing out there."

"Glad to do it. I brought you a surprise." He ignored her "you-shouldn't-have's," retrieved the picture from the foyer where he'd left it and rested the bottom edge of the frame on the sofa. "Dad, could you help me with this?"

"Certainly." His father stepped forward.

With his father's assistance Liam removed the paper. The memory of doing the same with Aubrey yesterday barged front and center into his thoughts. He set his jaw and deliberately blocked the images as best he could. Which wasn't so great.

His mother's gasp was reward enough for the weeks of phone calls Liam had made to nearly every gallery in the Northeast, his pleas with gallery owners and, finally, the letter he'd written to Gilda Raines and sent along with a picture of his mother gazing at one of Gilda's paintings in the medical center. Seeing his mother's eyes light up and then fill with happy tears was icing on the cake.

She smiled up at him. "Gilda Raines never sells anything. She donates to hospitals, but she *never* sells. How did you convince her?"

He shrugged. "I wrote her a letter and told her I needed a gift for a very special lady."

"Don't waste your flattery on me, Liam Elliott." His mother dismissed his words with a wave of her hand, but color seeped into her cheeks.

He didn't mention that the artist probably wouldn't have sold him anything if Aubrey hadn't been with him. He'd seen the refusal in Ms. Raines's eyes until Aubrey had remarked about the painting being exactly what Liam's mother needed. He knew because he'd been looking at Gilda instead of the art on the easel.

Liam had a feeling he was supposed to know why the artist had selected this particular piece from her collection and what the painting signified the second he laid eyes on it, and when he hadn't Gilda's decision had been made. No sale. But Gilda had taken an instant liking to Aubrey, and Aubrey's promise to explain the meaning behind the morning glory had changed Gilda's mind. No doubt about it. He would have walked away empty-handed if not for Aubrey Holt. He owed her. Even the gallery manager had whispered her surprise over the sale—when she'd slipped him her phone number. Not a number he intended using.

His mother carefully eased forward on the cushion until she could stroke the frame. "It's beautiful. Absolutely beautiful."

Tears streamed from her eyes and she pressed trembling fingers to her lips. Those were more than happy tears this time. Liam stood by helplessly, but his father immediately took her into his arms and tucked her face to his chest. Did his mother's emotional reaction have something to do with the way Aubrey had described the painting? Liam's ears burned and he shifted uneasily. If so, then his parents deserved a moment of privacy.

He propped the frame against the back of the sofa, shoved his hands into his pockets and retreated to the opposite side of the room to look out the window at the Brooklyn Heights neighborhood where he'd grown up. Until he'd moved away, he hadn't paid much attention to the well-maintained nineteenth-century brownstones lining the shaded street, the wide bluestone sidewalks or decorative ironwork. He hadn't appreciated that he was only a short train ride from Times Square, Coney Island and Shea Stadium and a Mets baseball game.

While he'd been trapped under the weight of family expectations, his thoughts had been elsewhere. Traveling. Exploring. With his grandfather owning Elliott Publication Holdings, one of the largest and most successful magazine conglomerates in the world, it had been assumed for as far back as Liam could remember that each family member would start with EPH and work his or her way up. Liam hadn't even left the area to attend college. Instead he'd commuted to Columbia University on the Upper West Side of Manhattan and interned at EPH, working hard to climb the EPH ladder.

Liam didn't like to make waves. As a second son, he was a peacemaker not a troublemaker.

Until yesterday.

Yesterday would cause all kinds of trouble if word of his after-lunch activities got out.

"I want to hang it in the bedroom." His mother's statement interrupted his thoughts.

"Just show me where," his father answered in an indulgent I'll-give-you-anything-you-want voice. "Could you help me, son?"

"Sure."

Carrying the painting, Liam followed his parents into their bedroom. His father helped his mother settle on the bench at the end of the bed. She glanced around the room and then pointed. "I want to hang it there, so it'll be the first thing I see each morning and the last thing before I turn out the light."

TMI. Too much information. Aubrey's description echoed in Liam's head and his skin shrank three sizes. *Don't want to go there.* His parents' intimate life was none of his business and Liam liked it that way.

His father removed the landscape already hanging on the wall and replaced it with the morning glory.

"Perfect," his mother announced.

His father hooked an arm around Liam's shoulders and nodded toward the painting. "This was a great idea."

Liam glanced at his mother. She studied the art with her hands clasped under her chin and a smile on her face. And then he turned back to his father. "So do you know what it means?"

His father shifted uncomfortably and lowered his arm. "Only because your mother fell in love with one of the paintings by this artist hanging in the hospital physical therapy room. I asked what was so great about a picture of a flower and Renee explained it to me."

Renee was the social worker engaged to Tag, Liam's younger brother. They'd met when Renee was assigned to keep Tag from terrorizing the hospital staff caring for their mother after her double mastectomy.

Liam shared a sympathetic look with his father and then confessed, "I had to have somebody explain it to me, too."

His father crossed to the dresser and returned with a pair of gilt-edged tickets in his hand. "While I have you here I need a favor. There's a charity thing this weekend. Your mother and I have decided to skip it, but we need an Elliott to make an appearance. Saturday night. Black tie. You'll need a date. Can you swing it?"

Aubrey's violet eyes flashed in Liam's mind. No. Definitely not Aubrey. He'd come up with someone who had Saturday night free and a spare formal hanging in her closet. "Sure."

"Good."

"So, how about you put the champagne on ice and I dash down the street and pick up dinner at Mom's favorite restaurant?" Liam suggested.

How in the hell he'd find a date on such short notice he didn't know. He'd been out of the dating circuit since his grandfather's announcement in January. But that wasn't his father's problem. If his parents wanted an Elliott at the gala, then Liam would be there, doing his duty the way he'd always done.

Aubrey looked at the man beside her and longed for a bed, a thick pillow, a silk-covered down comforter and solitude. Not sex. Which made her immediately think of Liam Elliott.

She huffed an exasperated breath and checked her diamond-faced watch. How long had she lasted this time? Less than an hour since she'd last vowed to never again think about Liam or their afternoon of amazing, curl-her-toes sex. God, she was weak. Blame it on exhaustion. She'd had precious little sleep during the past five nights, and when she had fallen into bed, Liam Elliott had joined her, invading her dreams and tangling her sheets.

Damn him.

As if thinking about Liam incarnated remnants of that afternoon, Aubrey spotted Trisha Evans across the ballroom. The gallery employee hadn't known that Aubrey and Liam weren't a couple, but that hadn't stopped her from brazenly passing Liam her phone number along with a come-and-get-me smile and his receipt.

Witch.

The crowd shifted and Aubrey choked on her champagne when she recognized Trisha's escort. *Liam.* Well, he hadn't waited long to accept the brunette's invitation. Emotion churned in Aubrey's stomach. Anger? Jealousy? Whatever it was, it didn't belong. How could she be angry or jealous? She and Liam weren't—and never could be—a couple.

"Who's the chick?"

"Pardon?" Aubrey turned to look at the hulking football player who'd escorted her to the arts fund-raiser this evening. One of her father's magazines was doing a series of articles on Buck Parks and his recent retirement from the NFL. Her father had "suggested" Aubrey and Buck create a little buzz about the feature by appearing together at the gala.

"The brunette in the barely there red dress. You're glaring at her like you want to mash her face into the turf."

An apt description. "No one. She's no one important."

But at that moment Liam turned his head. His gaze lasered in on Aubrey from across the room and her breath jammed in her chest. He looked amazing in a tux. Suave. Sexy. *GQ*-gorgeous.

"Ah, now I get it."

Aubrey blinked and broke the connection with Liam. Looking away wasn't as easy as it should have been. She found sympathy in Buck's eyes. "Get what?"

"It's not her. It's him."

Was she completely transparent? "You're mistaken. He's the financial operating officer of Holt Enterprises' chief competitor. I can't be interested in him."

Buck grinned and dipped his head. "Who're you trying to fool, Aubrey?"

Buck was tall and built, smart and funny. He smelled good and filled out his custom-tailored tux to perfection. Why couldn't she get hot and bothered over him? But she didn't. She experienced no blip of her pulse when he said her name, no sweaty palms when he looked at her, no burning twist of her stomach when he touched her. The feeling—or lack thereof—was mutual.

Mischief danced in his eyes. "Wanna give him something to think about? Because he's on his way over here."

Aubrey's heart stopped and then slammed in a rapid jackhammer beat. "He is?"

"Yep. I can plant one on you. Long, slow, and I'll make it look deep and hot. He'll get the message."

If she weren't panicking, she'd appreciate the handsome ball player's offer, but at the moment she was on the verge of hyperventilating. If he covered her mouth with his, she'd suffocate.

Buck's big hand curled around her waist and he tugged her closer. "Last chance," he whispered against her jaw.

"Aubrey." Liam's hard voice sent a flash-fire of heat over her skin.

Gulping, she took a second to gather her scattered nerves, pasted what she hoped passed as a disinterested smile on her face and turned. "Good evening, Liam. Trisha. Are you enjoying the ball?"

Aubrey avoided Liam by focusing on Trisha's triumphant smirk. Buck's hands tightened on Aubrey's waist. She made a mental note to thank him later. He reached past her and offered his hand first to Trisha and then to Liam. "Buck Parks."

Trisha, evidently not satisfied with one big fish on the hook, fluttered her mascara-laden lashes at Buck and gushed her name and something inane about football. Aubrey's deafening pulse drowned most of it out.

"Liam Elliott." Testosterone crackled in the air as the men shook hands and then Buck's arm settled around her waist and hauled her close to his hard body. Her pulse didn't even hiccup.

Aubrey risked looking at Liam again.

"Mom loved the painting," was all he said. His unreadable expression gave nothing away.

"I thought she would."

And then his lips twitched. "She had me hang it in her bedroom. I didn't ask why. Don't want to know."

Aubrey's lips curved upward. "No. I bet not."

Then memories of Liam touching her, tasting her, filling her, wiped away her smile and set her legs to trembling. She had to get out of here or at least away from him. She couldn't leave the gala until she'd done as her father requested. *Dance, schmooze, get your picture taken by a few society reporters.*

"Well, it was good seeing you both, but I promised Buck a dance. Bye." And then she looked up at the former quarterback and silently pleaded for him to rescue her. Lucky for her, Buck was as quick with his thoughts as he was on his feet.

Getting the seats switched cost Liam fifty bucks. The fact that he'd paid money to torture himself with what he couldn't have didn't say much about his intelligence.

He deliberately stalled until after Aubrey and her date

were seated at the big, round table with three other couples before leading Trisha to their seats in the banquet hall adjoining the ballroom. Aubrey glanced up as he pulled out his date's chair. Her violet eyes widened and filled with horror and then the color and her polite smile slid from her face.

She jerked her gaze forward and sat stiffly erect. Liam settled beside her. Their shoulders brushed as he adjusted his chair, and her scent filled his lungs, bringing back a flood of incendiary memories. His thigh nudged hers beneath the crowded table and blood drained from his brain.

He recovered enough to introduce Trisha and himself to the other diners at the table and then turned to Aubrey and her date. The big lug with her had tried to crush Liam's hand earlier. Too bad it hadn't worked. Liam had done his own share of bone crushing during the exchange.

Aubrey cozying up to the quarterback is none of your business.

"You left something at my place," he whispered to Aubrey.

Her cheeks turned scarlet, confirming she'd not only heard him, she knew exactly what she'd left behind, but she didn't turn her head. In fact, she ignored him, which irritated the daylights out of him.

"Want it back?"

"No. Throw it out." Her reply was barely audible over the hum of conversation in the large room.

He waited until after the salads had been served. "Can't do that, sweetheart."

She dropped her fork. Within seconds a server had replaced it with a clean one and stepped back to hover. One bad thing about five-thousand-dollar-a-plate dinners was that the wait staff never went far. They hovered behind you, watching every move. Not that he intended to touch Aubrey—no matter how much he wanted to.

Parks stretched his left arm across the back of Aubrey's chair, clenching his fist and displaying his Super Bowl ring for Liam's scrutiny. The gesture blatantly staked a claim, riling Liam. Hard eyes met Liam's behind Aubrey's back. Liam set his jaw.

Buddy, if she were yours, she wouldn't have been in my bed.

Aubrey glanced at Liam and then swiftly turned to the man on her right. She said something, drawing Parks's attention.

Liam faced forward. *What in the hell are you doing, Elliott? Are you willing to fight for a woman you can't have?*

Belatedly he remembered his own date. Forgetting a woman who had groped his butt on the dance floor and whispered in explicit detail what she'd like to do to him later ought to be more difficult, but he'd done so easily. Trisha didn't get to him the way Aubrey did, and he had no interest in accepting Trisha's naughty invitation. On the other hand, he knew without a doubt that if Aubrey had made those suggestions—wise or not—they'd be halfway back to his apartment already.

Aubrey's off-limits. Back off.

But knowing he should back off didn't make him any less aware of the woman to his right for the remainder of the tasteless dinner and long-winded speeches. He couldn't have her, but he ached for Aubrey Holt with each pulse of his blood and each lung-filling breath. Duty had never been so onerous and desire had never been more difficult to ignore.

Four

"Are you alone? Or is the thug with you?"

Aubrey's heart stalled at the sound of the deep, slightly husky voice on the phone. "Liam."

She scrambled upright in her bed, clutching the sheet to her chest and squeezing the phone so tightly her fingers hurt. And then she recalled his question. "That's none of your business."

"You *are* alone."

"I didn't say that." She shoved the hair out of her eyes and squinted at her bedside clock. "It's midnight. Why did you call?"

"To tell you that you looked beautiful tonight."

Her lungs failed. The phone slipped in her grasp. She fumbled it back to her ear. "Thank you. So did Trisha."

She cringed at the jealousy in her voice.

"Did she? I didn't notice." His distracted tone made her want to believe him, but the man had gone out with a woman who'd been ballsy enough to pass him her number with Aubrey standing two feet away.

"You shouldn't have called, Liam."

"You wanted me to tell you how beautiful you looked with your watchdog standing by ready to stamp my forehead with his Super Bowl ring?"

"Have you been drinking?" He sounded sober. Tired, but sober.

"Haven't had a drop since that lousy wine at dinner. But I couldn't get to sleep."

She knew the feeling. "So you decided to call and wake me?"

"Did I?"

"Did you wake me?" She should lie and say, yes, she'd been sleeping dreamlessly. But she didn't. "No."

She scooted back under the covers and laid her head on her pillow. She shouldn't ask, but her mouth didn't listen to her mind. "Why can't you sleep?"

The sound of a heavy breath and the rustle of sheets traveled through the phone line. Aubrey closed her eyes and a picture of Liam naked and kneeling above her on his king-size bed filled her head. She lifted her lids and turned on the lamp. Listening to Liam's sandpaper voice in the darkness and remembering him naked wasn't a good idea if she wanted to sleep any time in this century.

"I couldn't sleep because I was thinking about you. About Monday afternoon."

Her heart would very likely sustain permanent damage from its frantic battering against her rib cage. Her fingers crushed the sheets. She bit her lip.

"It was good."

"Good?" she choked out in disbelief.

His low chuckle made her shiver. "Better than good. Fabulous."

She smiled. "That's more like it."

"Incredible. Stupendous. Phenomenal." She could hear the laughter in his voice and then another rustling sound. "And it's a crying shame that it can't happen again."

Her grin faded at the seriousness and accuracy of the last statement. "But it can't."

"I know. But I don't have to like it."

Neither did she. "No."

The silence stretched for a dozen heartbeats. "Good night, Aubrey. Sweet dreams."

"You, too, Liam. Sweet dreams." She cradled the phone, turned off the light and then rolled on her side and tucked her hand beneath her cheek.

Odd phone call. So why was she smiling?

Seeing Liam again was out of the question. If she did, her father would expect her to weasel information out of Liam about EPH and she just couldn't stomach the duplicitous role. Her father had been angry enough that she hadn't brought him anything useful after her lunch with Liam. Oh, Matthew Holt hadn't yelled. He never yelled. But he'd treated her to that same silent stare she'd come to know so well.

She couldn't continue letting her father down. She'd worked her fanny off to be the kind of employee and daughter of whom he could be proud and she'd failed. She owed him for taking her in when he hadn't wanted her. He hadn't wanted custody during the divorce from her mother, and he hadn't wanted custody after Aubrey's jerk of a stepfather had crawled into her bed and offered to keep her from getting lonely while her mother was out of town.

Aubrey had heard her father arguing with Jane after she'd revealed that dreadful secret. His bellow had carried through his closed office door. "What in the hell am I going to do with a teenage girl?"

Aubrey hadn't heard Jane's reply. In fact, Aubrey hadn't heard anything from either of her parents until hours later when her mother had stormed into Matthew Holt's office with Aubrey's belongings and dumped them on the floor. She'd glared at Aubrey and said, "Look what you've done with your lies," and then left.

Pamela Holt Curtis hadn't asked for Aubrey's side of the story. She'd chosen to believe her young husband's version. He'd claimed Aubrey had invited him into her room and that she'd been flirting with him for weeks.

Aubrey had been left with a mother who no longer wanted her around and a father who had never wanted her in the first place.

"Liam."

Liam blinked his unfocused eyes and looked up from the papers on his desk to the man rapping on his office door. Cade McCann, the executive editor of *Charisma,* EPH's high-fashion magazine, also happened to be Liam's good friend, probably his best friend.

"Got a minute?"

"Sure, Cade. Come in." Considering Liam's mind had been elsewhere since this morning's monthly meeting with the editors in chief of the different magazines, Cade wasn't interrupting anything. Liam hated the tension invading the formally congenial meetings.

This week he'd been distracted by thoughts of Aubrey and he'd barely managed to relate the pertinent facts and figures. For a split second Liam considered asking Cade how to wipe a woman from his brain, but nixed the thought. His friend hadn't been too successful on that score, a fact proven by his recent engagement.

"What brings the rooster out of the henhouse?" The

question was a running joke between them. Cade was a rare male on *Charisma*'s predominantly female staff. A lesser man would have been henpecked into submission, but not Cade.

"Are you having woman troubles?" Cade asked as he settled in the chair in front of Liam's desk.

Alarm straightened Liam's spine. "Why do you ask?"

"Because I called you three times before you answered."

Liam silently swore. His mind had been on Saturday night and the phone call he shouldn't have made. Pretty damned stupid of him to throw fuel on a fire he was trying to put out. "What's up, McCann? Spit it out."

Cade's direct gray gaze said he wasn't fooled by Liam's evasion. "Okay, if you want to play it that way. You'll have to lay your cards on the table eventually."

"Cade—"

"I want you to be my best man when I marry Jessie next month."

Jessie Clayton was the *Charisma* intern who just happened to have stunned them all with the revelation that she was Aunt Fin's daughter—a daughter Fin had been forced to give up for adoption twenty-three years ago. Until Jessie had revealed that shocking secret, Cade had questioned her loyalties and suspected her of being a plant from another magazine.

No doubt about where Aubrey Holt's loyalties lay. Liam rolled his shoulders, but the knot at the base of his neck didn't ease. "I'd be honored to stand up with you, Cade. Being your best man means I get to give you one hell of a bachelor party."

"I'm all for that. Jessie might not be. But no naked women. I have the only one I'm interested in looking at."

"What about the rest of us?"

Cade leaned forward, bracing his elbows on his knees and clasping his hands. "Want to talk about her?"

Her. Cade didn't mean Jessie. "You're offering to *give* me dating advice? Last month you were *asking* for it."

Cade snorted. "And some good you were."

"Hey, I told you to go for it."

"Well, I'm telling you the same thing. Last month I was battling the current and trying not to get sucked into the love whirlpool. Looks like you might be in the water this month. Don't fight it, man. Let it pull you under. You'll be glad you did."

Love? Hell no. He'd only spent a few hours with the woman. But lust? Oh, yeah. He had a bad rash of that and it itched 24/7. "I can't."

"Why not?"

"She's—" Damn. He hadn't meant to let that slip. "Because the only problems I'm having are EPH problems. She's been a bitch of a mistress since January, compliments of Patrick and his damned competition."

Cade shook his head. "You're lying through your pearly whites, pal. When you want to talk, let me know. In the meantime, see if you can clear your calendar for the weekend after this one. Jessie's father's throwing us an engagement party in Colorado next Saturday. I'd like you to be there. I don't want to be the only city slicker on the ranch."

Liam looked at the stacks of files and reports on his desk. With his workload, dropping everything and flying to Colorado sounded insane, but it might be worth it if putting some mileage between him and a certain female could get her out of his head. "I'll be there."

"I'm heading for the cafeteria. Coming?"

"No, I have an errand to take care of." A fool's errand.

Aubrey stood in front of her father's desk, feigning calm she didn't feel. Why had he requested this late afternoon meeting?

He kept her waiting while he scanned the blueline in front of him. Checking the magazine proof was the production manager's job, but her father tended to spend a lot of time looking over everyone's shoulders—especially hers. He second-guessed each decision she made, which made the rest of the staff do the same. He claimed he hadn't gotten to the top by letting others do all the dirty work, and delegating wasn't something he enjoyed.

Finally, she asked, "You called?"

He put the blueline aside, revealing the folded newspaper beneath it. Aubrey's tension eased. She suspected he'd seen the photo in the society section. He should be pleased. She and Buck Parks had done exactly as he'd requested and garnered a little free publicity from not only the newspapers but a few celebrity magazines as well.

But that wasn't an approving smile on her father's face.

"You sat beside Liam Elliott at the dinner. What did you learn?"

She concealed a wince. Yes, Liam's face was easily recognizable in the picture. She'd hoped her father wouldn't notice. "Um, nothing. Buck was my date. I talked to him, not to Liam Elliott."

In fact, she'd done her best to ignore Liam throughout the mediocre meal and the soporific speeches afterward. Her best hadn't been good enough. She'd been hyperaware of each shift of his body. And any change in the ventilation of the stuffy banquet hall had wafted his cologne in her direction. As if that weren't bad enough, his phone call Saturday night had only worsened her preoccupation. Warmth swept through her at the memory. She bit her lip and vowed once again to quit thinking about him.

Very slowly her father lowered the paper. "You missed your chance at lunch. You could have redeemed yourself at the gala. How many times do I have to tell you? Never let an opportunity to find out what the competition is doing slip by."

A heavy blanket of failure settled over Aubrey's shoulders. "Yes, sir, I understand. But Liam Elliott is tight-lipped about EPH. You couldn't pry him open with an oyster knife. I can't—"

"There is no such thing as *can't,* Aubrey. Something is going on at EPH. Patrick Elliott runs a first-class armada."

He extracted a page of handwritten notes from one of the neat piles on his desk. "Patrick's son Michael has been out of the office more than he's been in while his wife has undergone chemotherapy. Michael's oldest son is running *Pulse.* Patrick's second son, Daniel, has stepped down as editor-in-chief of *Snap* magazine in favor of his youngest son. Patrick's daughter, Finola, suddenly has had a secret offspring emerge from the woodwork, and Elliott's granddaughter—one of the twins—has taken off with a rock star and left her ex-fiancé engaged to her sister."

He lowered the paper and focused hard eyes on Aubrey. "That's only the news my clipping service has found in the papers. For this many ships to be adrift in Elliott's port there must be a storm stirring the water. I want to know what kind of storm and when it's expected to make landfall. Find out."

Flabbergasted, Aubrey gaped at him. "I'm the VP of single copy sales not an investigative reporter."

"I've given you a direct order, Aubrey. You know Liam Elliott. Use him as your inside contact."

Use him. "I—I don't think I can help you."

"I didn't ask you to think. Do it," he commanded in an end-of-discussion tone.

My family's in enough turmoil without throwing an affair with the enemy's daughter into the pot. Liam's comment echoed in Aubrey's head. Her father's obvious disappointment in her tempted her to throw out this tidbit to prove that she wasn't a complete failure, but she was no Mata Hari who slept with men and then shared their secrets.

"I'll see what I can find out." But she wouldn't— couldn't—go back to the source. Advertising sales directors maintained high-level contacts within advertising agencies. She'd speak to Holt Enterprises' sales directors and get them to pump the clients they shared with EPH. If there was anything amiss at EPH, maybe some of the advertisers had noticed. And then she'd collate that info and report back to her father. That way she wouldn't be sharing anything Liam had told her in confidence.

Asking for the report still felt dirty, though.

Her father turned back to the proof, dismissing her without words—an all too familiar experience. Aubrey headed for her office. There were days she hated her job. This was one of them. She reached the threshold of her office and stopped in surprise. An exquisite floral arrangement in a crystal vase sat on her desk.

Roses and Asiatic lilies in the palest pink filled her office with a heavenly scent. Who would send her flowers? Other than the obligatory bouquet her father sent on her birthday, which had been months ago, she never received flowers. She hurried forward and inhaled deeply before extracting the card buried in the lush greenery. Aubrey slid a fingernail beneath the envelope's sealed flap and extracted the card.

"The color of the flowers reminded me of your dress and their fragrance reminded me of you. Thanks again for your help with the painting. L."

Liam. Her dress for the gala had been beaded pink silk. He remembered. Aubrey pressed a hand over her racing heart. She glanced at the bold handwriting and then scooted behind her desk and dug in her purse for the business card she had yet to throw away. The bold script was identical. He'd written this note himself rather than anonymously phone it in to a florist. Why that mattered she didn't know.

Don't turn this into something romantic, Aubrey. It isn't and can't be.

Now what? Should she e-mail Liam and thank him for the flowers? She didn't dare do that from here where all incoming and outgoing e-mail was saved on a huge server, but she could from her personal computer at home. Maybe she should send a polite but distant thank-you note via U.S. Postal Service. Or should she call? Again, not from here and not the wisest choice since hearing Liam's voice weakened her knees and her resolve to resist him.

Until she could make up her mind, Aubrey tucked both cards in her purse and tried to keep the telling smile off her face.

Liam Elliott had no business sending her flowers.

And she had absolutely no business being tickled pink to receive them.

Why torture yourself? Do what she said. Throw the thong out and get some sleep.

But Liam didn't pitch Aubrey's lingerie into the trash. He lay in bed staring at the black satin in his hand.

He'd gone to bed early to try to catch up on some of the shut-eye he'd been missing, but so far all he'd done was toss and turn and fight the hunger thickening his blood and tightening his skin. Her scent clung to the lingerie. He pitched it onto the nightstand and then turned out the light and rolled over. The sheet clung to his overheated skin. He kicked it off, but it didn't help. Resting one hand beneath his head, he hunkered down for another night of staring at the ceiling.

What was it about Aubrey Holt that made her so damned hard to forget? Her violet eyes? Her slender figure? Her summer-roses scent? Or the way she'd driven him wild in bed? If he could understand her allure, then he'd be steps closer to eradicating her from his thoughts.

And what was it about him that always drew him to the wrong women? In college it had been his freshman academic advisor. He hadn't known she was married until after they'd been sleeping together for a month. He'd ended the affair immediately, a little older, a little wiser and a lot more wary. His junior year he'd become involved with a woman on the rebound. He'd lost his heart when she'd returned to the jerk who'd dumped her.

For some reason attached women sought him out. His sister, Bridget, claimed it was because he was a good listener. But, hell, problem solving was what he did best. He listened to both sides, weighed the evidence and then worked out a solution. Working out the solution was his favorite part—like solving a riddle. But he'd learned the hard way to find out a woman's marital status before asking her out.

Aubrey's single.

Don't go there, man.

The phone rang, jarring him, but he welcomed the interruption. He glanced at the bedside clock. Eleven. Probably Cade calling. He picked up. "Hello."

Silence greeted him. "Hello," he repeated.

"Liam."

The breathless voice sent his pulse rate soaring. Not Cade. "Aubrey."

"I'm sorry to call so late. Did I wake you?"

"No."

"Thank you for the flowers. They're beautiful." The words came out in a rush, as if she'd been practicing them for a while.

"You're welcome. They reminded me of you."

"You shouldn't say things like that."

"Probably not." No probably about it. And Aubrey shouldn't have been the first thing he thought of when he spotted the arrangement in the florist's window during his morning run. But she'd been in his head all week. Why would this morning be any different? He'd dashed to the florist at lunch to place the order when he should have stayed at EPH and eaten in the company cafeteria with Cade.

"Well… I should go. I just called to…well, thank you."

He didn't want to let her go. He reached for the thong, brushing his fingers over the satin. "What are you doing?"

"What?"

"What are you doing? Right now."

He heard a rush of air, as if she'd exhaled into the receiver. "Getting ready for bed."

"I beat you to it."

"Excuse me?"

"I'm in bed."

"Oh. Oh my God. Are you alone? Did I inter—"

"Aubrey, you didn't interrupt anything. I'm alone. You?"

"Am I alone? Of course…I mean, yes, I am."

A smile tugged his lips. "What are you wearing?"

"Liam. You shouldn't…" Her scandalized voice trailed off.

He'd crossed the line. He wouldn't be surprised if she slammed the receiver down.

"A white satin nightgown."

The image instantly filled his head. He bit back a groan. "Short or long?"

"Long." Another pause stretched between them. "What are you wearing?"

His heart thumped harder. "It's just me and your thong." What had possessed him to reveal that?

"You're wearing my thong!"

He rocketed up in bed, his body hot with embarrassment. "Hell no. I'm holding it. In my hand."

Her chuckle, low and sexy as hell, marched down his spine. "You had me worried for a minute."

"That I was a cross-dresser?"

"Yes. Are you?"

Was she yanking his chain? "God, no."

"Good. Not that it matters, since we're not seeing each other."

"No, we're not."

"I should go."

He scrambled for a way to detain her and recalled a comment she'd made at lunch before she knew his identity. "Did you want to run screaming from the building today?"

"You mean work? Yes. I'm having a lot of those days lately."

Was she lying in bed or seated on the edge? He wanted to ask, but didn't. "Same here."

"I'm sorry."

"Ditto." For once Liam wished he had someone to confide in. In the past he'd talked his problems through with his grandfather or Cade, but both were off-limits this time. His grandfather's plan was the cause of Liam's stress, and Cade worked for EPH and was, therefore, part of the trouble. Liam felt like a bone in the middle of a pack of starving dogs. Everybody wanted something from him, something he couldn't deliver. The staff. The advertisers.

He opened his mouth and then shut it again. Aubrey worked for the competition. Not a safe sounding board.

"Any chance your week will improve?" she asked.

"Doubtful. I'll be working through lunch all week."

"Maybe next week will be better."

It wouldn't unless his grandfather cancelled this damned

contest. "Hope so. And I hope yours is, too. Good night, Aubrey. I'm glad you called."

"Me, too. Good night, Liam. I won't say, 'See you around' because I won't."

"No. Guess not." And for some reason, that disappointed him.

A rainy day had its advantages.

The inclement weather forced Liam to relocate his usual morning run to the executives' section of EPH's private gym—the one place he could be certain to find his grandfather before the workday began. Since Liam needed to talk to Patrick, he could handle the two chores simultaneously, efficiently. Privately.

Judging by the sweat ringing the neck and underarms of his grandfather's T-shirt, Patrick must have been on the treadmill for a while. It was only 5:30, but his grandfather had started early. As usual, the TV in front of the machines streamed CNN.

Liam hoped he was as sharp as Patrick mentally and physically when he hit seventy-seven. Then again, maybe his grandfather was slipping. This retirement selection process wasn't a smart move.

Liam stepped onto the treadmill beside Patrick's as he'd done dozens of times before. The room, thankfully, was empty except for the two of them. "Morning, Patrick."

"Liam." Patrick didn't slow his stride.

Liam worked up to his optimum speed. Once his muscles loosened and he'd reached a comfortable pace he decided to broach the subject that had been keeping him up at night.

The other subject. No way would he discuss with his grandfather his nonrelationship with Aubrey Holt.

"Your contest is tearing EPH apart. You have to end it."

"Not time yet."

"Yesterday's meeting was a combat zone."

"EPH will be stronger once we're done," Patrick said with conviction. Or was it just stubborn pride?

Liam made a conscious effort to unfurl his fists. "Not if the team disbands. We're fighting ourselves instead of the enemy, Patrick. It's only a matter of time before our advertisers pick up on the infighting."

Patrick turned a hard eye on Liam. "The enemy. Holt."

Liam's neck prickled. "He's not our only competition."

"Your grandmother showed me the picture in the paper. Unfortunate error, the hostess seating you beside Holt's daughter."

If Patrick found out that error had cost Liam fifty bucks, his grandfather would hit the ceiling. For Patrick Elliott appearances were everything and consorting with the enemy never looked good. Liam said nothing. Instead he increased his pace and directed his attention to CNN.

Minutes later Patrick turned off his machine and Liam did the same even though he hadn't yet reached his usual distance. "Patrick, I don't know if the family relationships will survive this contest. We're cutting each other's hearts out. Reconsider. Please."

"I've set a course. I'll see it through." Patrick wiped the sweat from his face with a white towel bearing the EPH monogram.

"No matter what the costs?"

"No matter what the costs."

"You're making a mistake."

"I don't think so, son, and I'm willing to wager the company on that."

"Good, because that's what you've done. I hope you don't live to regret it." Hoping to ease his frustration, Liam climbed back on the treadmill and set himself a mind-numbing pace.

* * *

"Your lunch is here."

Liam looked up from the spreadsheet. He hadn't ordered anything. Ann, his administrative assistant, must have. "Thanks, Ann. Put it there. I'll get to it as soon as I finish this."

She set a bag on the corner of his desk. The Ernie's Pub logo on the receipt caught Liam's attention, slamming his train of thought against a wall. Nobody at EPH knew about his penchant for Ernie's—an intentional omission. "Could you close the door on your way out?"

Her eyebrows rose. He never closed the door unless he had a private meeting. "Certainly."

As soon as the latch clicked he shoved his paperwork aside and reached for the bag and the receipt stapled to the outside. "Bookmaker's Special," he read. His favorite sandwich and he knew damned well no one in this building knew that.

His heart stuttered as he tore open the folded-down top and pulled out the ordinary Styrofoam container inside. The note taped to the top of the box wasn't in any way, shape or form ordinary. He ripped it off.

"Sorry you have to work through lunch. Enjoy. A."

Aubrey had sent him lunch.

He didn't know what to make of the gesture, but he sure as hell knew he shouldn't be smiling. He tried to wipe the grin off his face, but it returned. In the midst of the tension at work his and Aubrey's secret game was pure pleasure. Forbidden pleasure. He reached for the phone with one hand and his wallet with the other, planning to dig out her number, call her and thank her. But he set the phone back in the cradle and shoved his wallet back into his pocket.

He couldn't call her from here. He'd call her tonight.

Tonight when it would be just the two of them.

Five

Aubrey's phone rang, startling her into dropping her book into the bathtub. "Blast."

She snatched up the juicy and now soggy romance, pitched it onto the vanity, grabbed a towel and dashed for the phone extension in her bedroom. She was out of breath by the time she reached it. She glanced at the clock as she grabbed the receiver. Eleven. "Hello."

"You don't sound as if you were sleeping."

"Liam." Her knees buckled. She sank down onto the mattress, not caring if she dampened the linens. "No. I wasn't asleep."

"Are you alone?"

"Of c— Yes."

"You sound out of breath. Did I interrupt something?"

The wicked lilt in his voice made her heart blip erratically. What was he implying? "I was reading a book."

"And the book made you breathless? Must be a good one. Which book?"

As if she'd tell him that she read romances because in the stories a woman could be happy with one man forever, and love at first sight lasted for eternity—unlike her mother, who'd fallen instantly in love and married four times since divorcing Aubrey's father. The husband who'd made a pass at Aubrey had lasted less than two years, but by then Aubrey's relationship with her mother had been irrevocably changed. "I'm not reading anything you'd be interested in."

"How do you know?"

She sighed. "It's a romance, Liam."

"Ahh. A hot one?" The husky tone of his voice gave her goose bumps. No telling what he thought she'd been doing to make herself pant while reading the steamy book.

"I—I was in the tub. I had to run for the phone." Her skin flushed at the boldness of her confession.

A low groan carried through the phone line. "You fight dirty."

A laugh bubbled up her throat. He had no idea how unlike herself she'd behaved since meeting him—or at least the self she'd been since joining her father's company. It was all Liam's fault. He made her feel sexy and naughty, and he made her want to break rules for once in her life and say to hell with pleasing her father.

"Should I let you get back to your book?"

"It'll have to dry before I can finish it."

"Why?"

She cringed. "Because I dropped it in the tub when the phone rang."

"Give me the title. I'll replace it."

"You don't have to do that. I'm the klutz, not you."

"I've seen you dance. You're no klutz. Aubrey…" he said,

his voice lowering into a commanding tone that sent shivers up her spine "…give me the title."

She reluctantly relayed the information. "But you don't have to replace it. It will be fine once the pages dry out. And I can't keep receiving gifts from you at work."

"You're going to get me in trouble," he voiced her thoughts before she could.

"How am *I* going to get *you* into trouble? All I sent was a sandwich. You sent the most amazing bouquet. All the admins are talking." Aubrey absently blotted the droplets on her shoulders with her towel.

"The atmosphere at EPH is…tense, but your lunch surprise had me smiling all afternoon. The staff probably wonders what I'm up to. Thanks for sending the sandwich."

"You're welcome. I hope the rest of your week improves."

"Yours, too. Anything I can do to help?"

She gulped. *Yes, spill your guts about EPH's problems and then give me permission to share the information with my father.* "I think I have it under control."

Silence stretched between them. Aubrey didn't want to hang up, but she couldn't think of a thing to say to keep him on the line. Why did this man have the power to make her tongue-tied?

"You know where I live. How about you even the score?"

Her fingers contracted on the damp towel. "I'm around the corner on Fifth, only a couple of blocks up from you."

"That close?"

"Yes."

"We could meet—"

"No, Liam, we can't." But she wanted to. She really, really wanted to.

"Right. I should say good night and hang up, but I know if I do I'll just lie here and think about you. Tell me how to stop thinking about that afternoon, Aubrey."

Her breath jammed in her throat. "I can't. Because I'm having the same problem. Do you think it's just the taboo thing? Wanting what we can't have?"

She wouldn't know. She always dated men her father would approve of.

"Maybe. Probably. I don't know. You said I got you out of the tub. You must be cold."

Cold? No, her skin burned. It was a wonder the remaining droplets on her skin didn't sizzle like butter in a hot pan. "I'll get back in when we're finished."

"Why wait? Do you have a portable extension?"

She bit her lip. "You want to talk to me while I'm in the tub? Is this going to turn into an obscene phone call?"

His seductive laugh warmed her even more. "Do you want it to?"

Aubrey pressed a hand to the booming in her chest. "I'm not sure. I've never had one."

"Good to know."

"Have you? Had an obscene call, I mean?"

"No. But it might be interesting."

She twisted the corner of the towel in her fingers. "Maybe. If it wasn't icky and if the person making it wasn't a psycho or a thirteen-year-old boy."

"Good night, Aubrey. You'll be hearing from me soon." And then he disconnected.

She slowly replaced the receiver. What did he mean, she'd hear from him? The book? Or would he call again? She was ashamed to admit she hoped he'd call. She loved listening to Liam's voice. And she really enjoyed knowing he was having as much trouble forgetting their lovemaking as she was.

Not lovemaking. Sex. And no matter how much she wanted more, a steamy memory was all it could ever be. Her father would never forgive her for sleeping with a rival, and as long as she worked for Holt Enterprises and lived in a family-owned apartment, she had to follow her father's rules.

Twenty-nine and still following Daddy's rules. There was something pitifully not right about that.

"What a bitch of a day," Liam muttered as he poured himself a glass of wine and took a healthy sip.

Leaning against the kitchen counter, he rolled the rich pinot noir around in his mouth, savoring the cherry bouquet and smooth finish. He finished half a glass before the calming effect of the heavy red wine kicked in, soothing his jagged nerves.

This afternoon he'd fielded a flurry of calls from advertisers wanting to know if there were problems within EPH and demanding assurances Liam couldn't give them. What had tipped them off to the internal strife? Patrick had all but levied a gag order on the company employees, but there had to be a leak somewhere. Having the advertisers get fidgety could cause EPH's advertising revenues to drop. He'd have to speak to the sales managers and remind them to keep EPH's internal dissention to themselves.

The clock on the microwave revealed the late hour. Liam had worked through lunch and dinner. Cooking didn't appeal. Going out appealed even less. But he had to eat because he had plans for later that required him to keep his mind sharp. His pulse quickened in anticipation. At the same time his stomach knotted. His plan was unwise. Foolish.

Fun.

He pulled a frozen casserole from the freezer and shoved it into the microwave. An executives' catering company supplied him with precooked meals for the nights he was too tired to cook. The service provided all the benefits of having a personal chef without having anyone underfoot in his apartment. And if he had a hot date he had the option of having the chef prepare a gourmet meal and clear out before his company arrived. Not an option he'd used yet.

While his dinner defrosted he settled on a bar stool at his granite kitchen counter, sipped his wine and studied the bottle and the label. Louret Winery, a small outfit in Napa Valley, California, had become one of Liam's favorite producers since he'd discovered their wines last year. He promised himself a tour of the facility as soon as the dust settled at EPH. As far as he was concerned, that date couldn't come soon enough.

An hour later he'd eaten, showered the knots from his shoulders. Now he sat beside the phone with his heart thumping a wild beat and a different kind of tension tightening his muscles. Adrenaline flowed through his veins as the clock inched toward midnight. As soon as the hands hit twelve he punched out the number.

"Hello?"

His pulse nearly deafened him to Aubrey's soft voice. "This is an obscene phone call. Hang up if you're not interested."

He heard Aubrey gasp, but she didn't sever the connection.

"Are you alone?" he asked in as low and sexy a voice as he could manage—not difficult considering his throat had closed up.

"Yes. Are you?"

"Not anymore." A crazy answer. Of course he was alone, but having Aubrey on the line made him feel less lonely—an emotion Liam had experienced far too frequently since Patrick's contest made him all too often the unwelcome messenger bearing bad news. "What are you wearing?"

"A smile."

His brain nearly imploded. He gulped his wine. "Anything else?"

"A nightgown."

"You're a tease, Aubrey Holt. What color?"

"Black."

Liam groaned. "Details, please."

She hesitated so long Liam feared the game he'd antici-pated since last night was over. "Long with spaghetti straps and a lace bodice. There are sheer bits on my—"

"Wait," he groaned. His control wavering, he took another sip of wine. "Let me savor that much before you send me into overload with more." He closed his eyes and pictured Aubrey dressed as she'd described, in a puddle of black filmy fabric lying on his cream-colored sheets, waiting for him. And he ached. His body pulsed and throbbed, growing heavy with need. A saner man would take a cold shower or take matters into his own hand. "I'm ready. Where are the sheer bits?"

"Guess."

Her answer surprised a laugh out of him. "I need a hint. High or low?"

"High."

"If I were with you, could I see your breasts? Your nipples?"

"Yes."

Liam fisted his hand in his hair and took an unsteady breath. "You definitely fight dirty."

"What are you wearing?"

"Boxers. Silk. Blue." And they'd suddenly become tight. Very, very tight.

"No thong?"

He grinned, opened the nightstand drawer and extracted the garment. He stroked the smooth satin between his fingers. "No. That's in my hand. It smells like you, but your skin is softer, warmer."

Her gasp filled his ear. "You're good at this obscene phone call business."

"I could get better with practice."

"Are we going to practice?" Was that a hopeful note in her voice?

Should he continue this insane game, continue to lose sleep and drive himself to the aching edge of need again and again? "I'd like to."

"Me, too."

If he didn't change the subject he was going to lose what was left of his sanity and the call would go from sexy to raunchy. "Was today better than yesterday?"

"You mean at work?" Her sigh carried over the phone lines. "Not really. Sometimes I wonder if I should quit and find a job where I don't have to work so hard to prove myself."

The frustration in her voice came across loud and clear. "What happened?"

Seconds ticked past. "My father assigned me a task. I called a staff meeting and explained what I needed. But no one listens to me. They all think I was given my job because of my father and not because I earned it."

"I don't have to worry about that with EPH. Patrick made each of us pay our dues by working our way up through the ranks."

"I'm sorry, Liam. I didn't mean to ruin your call by whining."

"You're not whining, and I needed to change the subject before I asked you to take off your nightgown and touch yourself the way I would if I were there."

A half-choked sound carried over the line. "And would you return the favor? Touch yourself the way I want to?"

Desire churned thick and hot through his veins. He cursed. "Yes. Anywhere you want."

"Next time, then." And then he heard a click followed by the dial tone.

Next time. The words energized him, filling him with an anticipation for tomorrow that he hadn't felt in a long time.

Aubrey floated through her workday in a cloud of excitement, unwarranted by her position as VP of single copy sales. She'd breezed through phone calls with uncooperative distributors and meetings with the other circulation department staff. None of the usual daily irritations had brought her down or driven her for a double Mocha Frappuccino, her help-I'm-losing-it drink.

If only every day could be this enjoyable. She felt a twinge of unease. It was really pitiful that she sought, from a voice on the phone, the approval she couldn't get at work.

Since arriving home she'd showered and shampooed, given herself a manicure and pedicure all in preparation for her hot date with the telephone. She'd set her alarm for midnight, but she hadn't needed the annoying beep to wake her because there was no chance she'd drift off to sleep with this overdose of adrenaline flowing through her veins. She'd been watching the clock for what seemed like hours.

She stepped into the sexy teddy she'd darted out to purchase at lunchtime, tied the ribbon bows on each shoulder and brushed her hands over the lace covering her. The regret that Liam would never see the seductive garment dampened her excitement a little.

Finally it was time to call. Her heart raced and her mouth dried. She took a sip from the bottle of water on her nightstand, settled back against her mountain of pillows and dialed.

"Hello."

Goose bumps raced over her skin at the sound of Liam's voice. "This is an obscene phone call. Hang up if you don't want to listen."

Liam snorted. "Are you kidding? Do you know any guy

who would hang up if he had a beautiful woman promising to talk dirty to him?"

A smile twitched on her lips. His comment erased much of her nervousness. "I bought something very special for you today. I'm wearing it."

"She goes for the kill on the first line," he muttered in a barely audible tone. "Describe it for me," he said in a louder voice.

"It's lacy and sheer and very brief." *I can't believe you're doing this, A.*

"Tell me more." His pitch was lower, huskier.

Her nipples beaded and desire tangled low in her belly. "It's cut very high and very low. My legs are bare. And it's sheer and red. A teddy with a bow on each shoulder. One tug on each ribbon and..."

He groaned. "You're killing me, Aubrey."

Her inner rebel relished this brief interlude of feeling sexy and desirable and wanted. She'd never have the nerve to act as brazen face-to-face. "I want to talk about fantasies tonight. Tell me, Liam, in your secret fantasies where is the one place you'd like to make love but haven't?"

"At a Mets game," he replied without hesitation.

That jarred her right out of fantasy land. She'd never attended a baseball game, but she couldn't imagine finding a private place in Shea Stadium. "A Mets game."

"You?"

She shook away the disturbing image of crowds, stale beer and peanut shells. Did she dare confess her secret? "An elevator."

She heard the whistle of his breath. "That could be arranged."

"I know, and I think about your private elevator at night when I—" no, she would not confess that "—when I can't sleep."

"Untie the bows, Aubrey."

She did as he asked. The lace slid downward, temporarily

snagging on her erect nipples and then gliding into a puddle at her waist.

"If I were there I'd kiss you, taste you until you begged me to stop," he promised in a gravelly whisper that made her lightheaded.

A quiver started deep inside Aubrey and radiated outward. "What makes you think I'd ever ask you to stop?"

"Aubrey." Her name was half moan, half plea.

Her pulsed fluttered like a hummingbird's wings and she squirmed restlessly, aching for his touch. "What are you doing right now, Liam?"

"Wishing you were here. This is insane. I need to see you."

"We can't. My father and your grandfather would never forgive us."

"To hell with them."

Regret tightened Aubrey's throat, dousing the sparks of arousal that had flared within her the moment she'd begun her evening preparations. She wished she could believe she and Liam had a future together, but even if Liam didn't consider her father the enemy, Aubrey knew from her mother's multiple marriages that love at first sight was an illusion. What she had with Liam, though breathtakingly powerful and thought-consuming at the moment, would pass.

"Liam, what we have is temporary. Our families aren't."

And then she hung up.

She had to end this and she had to end it now. If he called tomorrow night she wouldn't answer her phone.

"I have your books and I'm holding them hostage."

Aubrey nearly dropped the phone when she heard Liam's voice. She quickly glanced out her open office door and exhaled when she spotted her administrative assistant's empty chair. A check of her watch revealed it was almost six. Linda must have left for the day. "You shouldn't have called here."

"I'm using a pay phone. No caller ID will trace the call back to me, and I used the automated directory instead of going through the Holt Enterprises operator. The ransom I'm demanding for the books is dinner."

So much for her plan to ignore him. Temptation nipped at her, but guilt took an even bigger bite. The preliminary report on EPH from the advertising department lay on her desk waiting to be read, edited and forwarded to her father. Aubrey shoved it into a drawer without reading it. Whatever the report contained was common knowledge among the advertising staff. She hadn't pried and hadn't gained the information using underhanded methods.

She still felt guilty.

Just say no, A. "We can't risk meeting in public."

"My place. I'll cook."

What happened to no? "Did you say books, plural?"

"I did. I have everything ever published by the author you mentioned, including an autographed copy of her recently released hardcover. But if you want them it's going to cost you. I need to see you, Aubrey."

Common sense warred with desire. "And you accused me of fighting dirty."

"I play to win, and I promise that if you join me tonight we'll both win. I'll be waiting in the elevator at seven o'clock. Carlos, the doorman, will give you the key." The dial tone sounded.

The elevator. Did that mean what she thought it did? Aubrey couldn't catch her breath. She lowered the receiver, pressed a hand to her chest and tried to calm down to no avail. Tremors of excitement and nervousness shook her.

Did she have the courage to accept Liam's challenge? There was only one way to find out.

* * *

Liam leaned against the mirrored elevator wall and sipped his champagne. Five after seven. Would Aubrey show or had he pushed too far too fast?

You shouldn't be pushing at all. You should be walking away. But he couldn't. Aubrey Holt had taken possession of his thoughts, and he couldn't evict her no matter how hard he tried. And he had tried.

His heart chugged slower, heavier as minutes dragged past and Aubrey didn't arrive. He'd learned that she was punctuality-conscious at their first meeting. If she were coming tonight she wouldn't be late. Disappointment weighted his shoulders. He ought to pack it in and carry back to his apartment the ice bucket standing in one corner of the elevator and the bouquet of red roses lying in the other. He'd bought a dozen roses—not because that was the tradition but because they'd met and made love the first time twelve days ago.

Romantic sap. You didn't make love, you had sex. Mind-boggling, cook-your-brain sex.

The elevator jolted and so did his heart, and then the doors glided open. Aubrey stood in the foyer, with nervousness filling her wide eyes and white teeth digging into her siren-red lipstick. She held her purse in front of her waist in a white-knuckled grip. Liam couldn't stop the grin spreading over his face—one of relief, happiness—as he took in her seductive attire.

A black wraparound dress hugged her slender waist and dipped low between her breasts. Skimpy high-heeled sandals put her eyes on level with his. And her hair was rumpled, as if she'd just crawled out of bed.

"Come inside, drop your bag and push the button for my floor."

She hesitated, her gaze roving over the ice bucket, the

roses and then him in a slow head-to-toe perusal. Her breasts rose and fell on a deep breath before she did as he asked. Her scent mingled with the heavier perfume of the roses. The elevator whizzed upward, leaving Liam's stomach behind. Or maybe the woman a yard away caused the roller-coaster effect.

Aubrey knotted her fingers in front of her. The hem of her dress, which he could see in a multitude of reflections, swished almost imperceptibly with the fine tremor of her body. He poured her a flute of champagne. Their fingers touched on the stem as she accepted the glass. His pulse stuttered and her breath hitched. "I'm glad you came."

"Me too. I'm sorry I'm late. I went home to change first."

Tension eased from his shoulders. He'd feared second thoughts had caused her tardiness. "It was worth the wait. You look incredible. Sexy as hell."

She swallowed the champagne in her mouth with a sudden and audible gulp and her cheeks flushed. "Thank you. You too."

"Thanks." He'd showered, shaved and yanked on pale gray slacks and a pullover sweater in a darker shade. Same routine he'd follow for any other date, but this wasn't like any other date. Tonight he was as nervous as a kid on prom night.

The elevator stopped on his floor and the doors opened. Liam made no effort to step out. Aubrey had said she fantasized about making love on an elevator, and he intended to fulfill that fantasy tonight—if she'd let him. The doors closed.

Her violet eyes found his and the awareness of his intent widened her pupils and quickened her breath.

Liam fought the hunger that urged him to grab her, yank the tie on the sexy dress to reveal the satiny skin beneath and then bury himself inside her. Hard. Deep. He used to have more finesse, more patience, but tonight a battle raged inside him.

Slow down.

"Decent day?" he forced out even though his mouth watered for the taste of her.

She rolled one shoulder. "As decent as it gets."

The telling flatness of her voice said more than her words. "You don't like your job."

She stared into her glass, swirling the pale liquid around and then sipping. "I'm good at what I do."

"But?"

Her troubled gaze met his. "But no, I don't enjoy my job."

"Why don't you leave?"

Another swirl of champagne. Another sip. "It's complicated."

"Try me. Tomorrow is Sunday and neither of us has to work. We have all night."

Her lips parted and then her pink tongue darted out to dampen them. "My father was there for me when I needed him. I owe him."

"Family duty is a heavy cross to bear." A fact he knew well.

"What would you do if you didn't work for EPH?"

If he didn't work for EPH... Not something he'd ever contemplated. "I don't know. Maybe try my hand at making wine."

"Making wine?" Her eyebrows arched in surprise.

He leaned against the brass rail separating the mirrored upper portion of the compartment from the dark wainscoting lining the bottom of the walls. Why did he feel comfortable confessing this to Aubrey when he'd never done so with his family or friends? "Wine's a hobby. I've been studying viticulture and enology for years."

She saluted with her now empty flute. "I don't know how much you've learned about growing grapes or making wine, but may I commend you on your taste in champagne?"

He nodded acceptance of the compliment. "Refill?"

The corners of her lips turned up. "Maybe later."

Liam's pulse beat as fast as a drum roll. He wanted to make love with Aubrey. No doubt about it. But he would have been happy to just have her company. He took her glass and set it beside his on the floor, and then he straightened. The desire in Aubrey's eyes slammed into him like a subway train, knocking the air from his lungs and the ability to think from his head. He lifted a hand and cradled her silky cheek. She leaned into his palm and her lids fluttered closed. A smile of pleasure curved her lips.

"I've been thinking about this since last night," he confessed, and then he kissed her, sinking into the damp softness of her lips and savoring the taste of Aubrey, a flavor uniquely hers combined with a nuance of the champagne.

He tunneled his fingers through her soft hair to cradle her nape and banded his opposite arm around her waist to pull her flush against him. Warm and pliant, she arched into him in perfect alignment. Her breasts teased his chest and the softness of her mound cushioned his erection.

Her arms wound around his waist and her fingers kneaded the tight muscles of his back. She angled her head, granting him deeper access, and hunger inflamed him. He shaped her shoulders with his palms, traced the line of her spine and the indention of her waist, and then he filled his hands with her tight, round bottom. A perfect fit.

Need rose inside him with overwhelming, suffocating strength. He raked his hands over her hips, down her thighs and then up again, carrying the hem of her dress with him. His fingertips encountered silken hose, an elastic band and a strip of bare skin. Stockings. He groaned into her mouth and traced the line of lacy elastic across the backs of her upper thighs. He explored higher and found nothing. Aubrey wasn't wearing panties or even a thong. Gasping for air, he yanked back his head and then he gritted his teeth as sexual heat pulsed through him with an urgency he'd never faced.

"You definitely fight dirty."

A smile quivered on her damp lips and mischief sparkled in her eyes. "I like to be prepared."

He eased a few inches between them and pulled the string fastening her dress at her waist. The rustle of the fabric ties against each other seemed unnaturally loud in the small compartment. He lifted both hands to cradle her face and kissed her again, fighting desperately to get a grip on his slipping control. He mapped the shape of her ears with this thumbs, smoothed over her fluttering pulse and then traced the V of her neckline. When he reached the valley between her breasts, he nudged the fabric aside and his knees nearly buckled.

Aubrey's tiny black bra only half-covered her breasts. The puckered tips were clearly visible beneath the border of the lacy cups. His mouth watered. His heart pounded. His lungs struggled to find sufficient oxygen in the suddenly airless elevator. Liam circled his thumbs over the lace, easing it aside, and then he dipped his head to take one tight tip into his mouth.

Aubrey whimpered and collapsed against the elevator wall. Her fingers tangled in his hair, holding him in place as he sampled first one breast and then the other, sipping, nipping, lightly abrading with his teeth.

His palms glided over the hot satin of her skin, outlining her waist and hips and then parting her dark tangle of curls, seeking and finding her moisture. Her gasps filled his ears, and her fingers tightened in his hair almost to the point of pain. Liam captured Aubrey's hands in his and transferred them to the cool, brass rail. "Hold on."

He took a moment to savor the sexy picture of Aubrey with her dress gaping open, her breasts damp above the skimpy push-up bra and her long, slightly parted legs encased in those sinful thigh-high stockings and stiletto heels. An aroused flush covered her face and chest, and desire kept her lids at half-mast.

He dropped to his knees, cupped her buttocks and tasted her. He stroked her with his tongue, filled his nostrils with the scent of her arousal and savored each whimper of pleasure he heard over the loud drumming of his heart. And then she climaxed. He supported her weight as pleasure undulated through her and then he rose, dug into his pocket for a condom and reached for his belt buckle with trembling hands.

"Let me," Aubrey whispered. Her fingers made quick work of his belt and pants, pushing them down his thighs. Good thing she worked fast since each brush of her fingers sent him closer to the edge of the cliff, and going over without her wasn't an acceptable option. She took the condom from him and smoothed it over his rigid flesh. All Liam could do was lock his muscles, grind his molars and battle his raging need.

"I need you inside me, Liam."

Her husky whisper nearly unmanned him. He'd never been happier to oblige a request in his life. He lifted Aubrey, rested her bottom on the brass rail and hooked her legs around his hips, and then he drove deep into the slick, hot glove of her body. Her arms twined around his neck, holding him close. For a moment he remained buried and still, as sensation engulfed him, and then he withdrew and plunged into her again and again until his lungs burned and his legs trembled.

Her lips found his, devouring him with one ravenous kiss after another until they were both gasping, and kissing became impossible. And then her head tipped back against the mirrored wall and she cried out his name. Her internal muscles clenched him and his own climax slammed through him.

He planted his hands against the mirror on either side of

Aubrey's head and lowered his forehead to the fragrant angle of her neck and shoulder. Satisfaction thickened and slowed his blood. "You smell delicious."

Her teeth caught his earlobe. "So do you."

And just that easily desire rekindled. How did she do it? How did Aubrey Holt turn him inside out and give him pleasure exponentially more satisfying than anything he'd experienced before?

It wasn't a question Liam could answer with his pants around his ankles and his brain lost in the ozone. Later, he promised himself, later he'd figure out why and how Aubrey knocked him sideways.

But first, he'd promised her dinner and a bag of books. And he always kept his promises. Always.

Six

She'd done it again.

Aubrey leaned back against the cool, mirrored elevator wall and tried to summon the guilt and regret she *should* be feeling for consorting with the competition. But she couldn't rally the negative emotions when every muscle in her body hummed with satisfaction, her heart still raced with passion and her arms and legs still encircled the man who'd fulfilled her secret fantasy. Liam's chest hair teased her breasts each time one of them inhaled.

The first time she and Liam had become intimate had been a fluke of hormones and happenstance, but this time she'd deliberately chosen to ignore her father's animosity for the Elliotts and pursue her own personal pleasure because Liam reminded her of the person she used to be. Fun. Sassy. A little naughty. Or at least that was what her college roommates at Radcliffe had claimed. Aubrey hadn't seen that girl in a long, long time.

Liam Elliott was the first person she'd ever met who understood the pressures of the family-owned magazine business, and their crazy late night calls had de-stressed her in a way that nothing else could. Not pills, nor alcohol. But an ongoing affair with Liam could be just as destructive to her job and her relationship with her father as a chemical addiction. She'd spent her entire life trying to please her father and prove her intelligence. This illicit involvement did neither of those.

"I guess avoiding each other isn't going to work," she asked once she caught her breath.

"Not a chance." Liam eased from her body and instantly she missed him. He helped her stand and then began righting her clothing. Her legs quivered unsteadily. Watching him make love to her in the mirrors had been hotter than she could believe, but his haste to redress her was quickly quenching that fire.

"Are you trying to straighten me up so you can shove me out the door?" She winced at the hurt in her voice and pushed his hands aside to complete the task, albeit unsteadily.

"No. But if I don't cover your delectable body, you're never going to get out of this elevator or get the dinner and books I promised you."

Pleasure wrapped around her like a warm blanket. "Oh. Well, in that case, may I return the favor?"

She bent her knees, intent on pulling up his slacks, but Liam caught her elbows and lifted her back up. "Not if you want to get out of here tonight. The thought of you on your knees…" He shook his head. "Hell, Aubrey, I can barely stand as it is."

His words and the desire lurking in his eyes sent her pulse into a tizzy. "Maybe later, then. What can I do for you now?"

"A loaded question." His eyes glimmered with suppressed hunger. He fastened his clothing, scooped up the roses and her purse and placed both in her arms. "The flowers are for you."

The heady scent of the flowers filled her nostrils. "Thank you. Florist roses don't usually have this much scent."

"I special-ordered them. Twelve, because twelve days ago we first did this."

His fingers tangled in her hair and he held her captive while he kissed her deeply, hungrily. By the time he released her lips, her head spun from lack of oxygen. Clutching the roses to her chest, she sagged against the elevator wall and filled her lungs with much-needed air.

Rendered speechless by the romantic gesture and his thoughtfulness, not to mention that killer kiss, she could only stare as he gathered the ice bucket and the champagne flutes and used his elbow to push the button to open the elevator doors.

Why oh why couldn't his last name be something besides Elliott? And why couldn't they have met and slowly fallen in love instead of instantly combusting?

The doors glided open. He nodded for her to precede him. Tantalizing smells greeted her as soon as he opened his apartment door. She followed him into the dining room. "Something smells delicious."

He deposited the ice bucket on a long cherry table that had been set with ivory cloth napkins, silver and crystal. "Steak Diane. Lucky for you, I'm pretty good in the kitchen."

"I imagine you're good just about anywhere." The bold comment—shades of the old Aubrey—slipped out before she could edit it.

Mischief sparkled in his baby blues, and the corners of his eyes crinkled as he pulled out a chair. "You're more than welcome to test that theory after dinner. Have a seat."

Aubrey laid the roses and her purse on the long table and

sat. Liam's hands briefly massaged her shoulders—just long enough to agitate her breathing—and then he bent to nuzzle a kiss on her nape. "I'll be right back."

After he left, Aubrey rested her head against the back of the chair. *What are you doing, A.? This path leads to a dead end.*

What's wrong with a dead end as long as you both know that's where you're headed?

Nothing, as long as hearts and hopes and hormones don't become entangled.

Liam made her feel young, energetic and sexy instead of old, neutered and dedicated only to her job. He relieved her stress and gave her amazing orgasms. What more could a girl want? She could be happy with that, couldn't she?

Absolutely. Without a doubt.

Hmm. Why did she have trouble believing that?

Because she wanted more. She wanted a loving husband, children, a home and a minivan. Despite her parents' bad examples, she knew there was such a thing as a happy marriage. Her college friends had married and started families. Aubrey frowned. She couldn't remember when she had last spoken to her friends. In the last few years work had taken over her life. Each time one of her friends had called she'd been shackled to her desk by some urgent deadline. She'd even given up her jogs in the park for a treadmill—with her laptop fastened to the handlebars—in her spare bedroom. Voice-recognition software made it possible for her to dictate her work as she ran.

Unfortunately, she could never have the American dream of 2-point-whatever children and a house with a yard with Liam. Even if it were possible to get over their Romeo and Juliet family situation, they'd met and ignited too quickly. Love at first sight—not that she imagined herself in love yet—wasn't based on anything deep and meaningful, and therefore it burned out quickly and painfully, and it left scars behind. Just look at her mother. Pamela Holt Dean Getty Richards Curtis paid more for therapy each month than Aubrey paid in rent and utilities combined.

The swinging door opened, interrupting her dark thoughts. Liam entered carrying a tray holding two plates and a small bowl. He set a plate before her. The other dish he placed in front of the chair at a right angle to hers and put the bowl between them. He discarded the tray, pulled a bottle of wine from the crook of his arm, efficiently uncorked it and poured the deep red liquid into the waiting goblets and then sat.

From the bowl he extracted a cloth and extended his hand. "May I?"

Surprised by this consideration, Aubrey placed her palm over his. Liam wrapped the warm, damp lemon-scented cloth around her hand and then embarked on the most sensual hand washing of Aubrey's life. He dragged the cloth between each finger, massaged her palm and the sensitive inner skin of her wrist, and then he repeated the process with her other hand. By the time he finished, the desire he'd so recently sated had rekindled and her breath came in short bursts. *All because he'd washed her hands.* She couldn't get over it. How did he get to her so easily?

He lifted his wine glass. "Enjoy."

"For as long as it lasts." She touched her glass to his with a *clink* of fine crystal and then sipped. Liam definitely knew his wines. Aubrey lifted her knife and sliced into the tender beef and then paused. "If we're going to have this…affair shouldn't we make some ground rules?"

"Good idea."

"No calls at work," she offered and then took a bite. The succulent meat melted in her mouth. "Delicious."

"Thank you. You're right. Calling at work was risky even

with the precautions I took. We need to keep our business and private lives separate. *Completely* separate," he stressed.

Guilt stabbed Aubrey between the shoulder blades. She washed down the lump in her throat with a gulp of wine. She had to destroy the report from the sales department. "Okay. And when either of us wants to end this, all we have to do is say so and that's it. No further contact. No questions asked. No explanations required."

"Agreed."

"No 'I love yous' or talk of the future. We both know this is temporary."

"Got it. Here and now. That's it."

A few moments passed as each ate in silence. Aubrey couldn't imagine being ready to say goodbye anytime soon, but then her mother probably never went into any of her marriages anticipating the messy divorces that followed, either.

She met Liam's gaze. "Meeting in public is out, and we can't meet at my apartment. My father owns the building and he lives in the penthouse above me. Besides the risk of running into him, there would be too many prying eyes. But a hotel seems…" She shrugged.

"Sleazy. My place is safe. My neighbor is overseas more often than he's home, and Carlos the doorman has been here forever. He's discreet."

Aubrey paused with her fork halfway to her mouth. "You mean there was no chance of us being interrupted in the elevator tonight?"

Liam's lips curled upward. "Not unless there was a fire, and, sweetheart, you came damn close to starting one. Watching you watch us…" He shook his head and then exhaled through pursed lips.

Warmth swept her cheeks at the compliment. "You could have told me sooner. About your neighbor, I mean."

The Silhouette Reader Service™ — Here's how it works:

Accepting your 2 free books and 2 free mystery gifts places you under no obligation to buy anything. You may keep the books and gifts and return the shipping statement marked "cancel." If you do not cancel, about a month later we'll send you 6 additional books and bill you just $3.80 each in the U.S., or $4.47 each in Canada, plus 25¢ shipping and handling per book and applicable taxes if any.* That's the complete price and — compared to cover prices of $4.50 each in the U.S. and $5.25 each in Canada — it's quite a bargain! You may cancel at any time, but if you choose to continue, every month we'll send you 6 more books, which you may either purchase at the discount price or return to us and cancel your subscription.

GET FREE BOOKS and FREE GIFTS
WHEN YOU PLAY THE...

Lucky 7

*Just scratch off the
silver box with a coin.
Then check below to see
the gifts you get!*

SLOT MACHINE GAME!

YES! I have scratched off the silver box. Please send me the 2 free Silhouette Desire® books and 2 free gifts for which I qualify. I understand I am under no obligation to purchase any books, as explained on the back of this card.

326 SDL EF4H   225 SDL EF4A

FIRST NAME   LAST NAME

ADDRESS

APT.#   CITY

STATE/PROV.   ZIP/POSTAL CODE

7	7	7	**Worth TWO FREE BOOKS plus 2 BONUS Mystery Gifts!**
🍒	🍒	🍒	**Worth TWO FREE BOOKS!**
♣	♣	♣	**Worth ONE FREE BOOK!**
🔔	🔔	🍒	**TRY AGAIN!**

www.eHarlequin.com

(S-D-10/06)

Offer limited to one per household and not valid to current Silhouette Desire® subscribers.

Your Privacy - Silhouette Books is committed to protecting your privacy. Our Privacy Policy is available online at www.eHarlequin.com or upon request from the Silhouette Reader Service. From time to time we make our lists of customers available to reputable firms who may have a product or service of interest to you. If you would prefer us not to share your name and address, please check here ☐.

DETACH AND MAIL CARD TODAY!

"And spoil your fantasy?"

A smile twitched on her lips. She'd never had a man ask her what her fantasies were, let alone go to such lengths to deliver one. She said a silent prayer of thanks that baseball season was over and she wouldn't be expected to play out his fantasy at the stadium. "Fantasies rarely live up to expectations, but this one did. You definitely didn't disappoint me."

"Glad to hear it."

And then Aubrey's blood chilled. "Oh my God. You don't have security cameras in the elevator, do you? I should have thought to ask before but I—"

His grin faded and he laid down his silverware. "We don't. Aubrey, you have my promise that I will never deliberately do anything to hurt or humiliate you."

Tension drained and panic subsided. That could have been a disastrous mistake. "Nor I you."

And she meant it. Her father would have to find another minion to investigate EPH.

Liam covered her hand with his on the table. His thumb stroked a trail of chaos along her inner wrist. "Do you have any idea how hard it's been for me to sit here knowing you're not wearing panties?"

Her appetite for food vanished and a hunger for Liam reawakened deep in her belly. She lowered her gaze from the fire in his eyes and surprisingly discovered her plate was empty. She barely remembered eating. "Let me help with the dishes."

She hastily snatched up her plate and his, rushed into the kitchen and unloaded them into the sink. After plugging the drain she turned on the water. Liam's arms bracketed her, caging her against the counter. He leaned forward until his chest pressed her shoulder blades and his erection rested in the crease of her bottom. His breath stirred the tendrils around her ear and she shivered. If it were possible for bones to melt, hers would be in a puddle on the granite floor.

"The dishes can wait. Join me in the shower. I want to get you wet."

She turned in his arms and pressed her hands to his chest. Her heart echoed the rapid beat of his beneath her palm. "I think you already have, but I'm willing to let you keep practicing if you insist."

For better or worse, her forbidden affair had begun.

Aubrey dropped her towel and reached for her dress. Liam snapped out of the sensual fog induced by the sight of her damp ivory skin. "Stay. Tomorrow's Sunday. No need to rush home."

She turned, chewing her bottom lip. "Are you sure?"

"Without a doubt."

Barely nine and they'd already had dinner and made love twice. She'd destroyed him, totally wrecked him, and five minutes ago after he'd come unglued in the shower he would have sworn he'd be sated for months to come. So why did hunger still gnaw at his veins? And why did the idea of waking up beside Aubrey make his body twitch to life?

She rested her palms on his chest, sifting through his chest hairs in a way guaranteed to make his soldier salute. He pressed his hands over hers, stilling her dangerous digits. Undeterred, she bent to sip a trail of kisses along his collarbone. He tangled his fingers in her damp hair and gently tugged her head back. "I thought you said you needed to rest."

Her siren's smile could tempt a saint—something he'd never aspired to be. "We'll rest awhile if you insist. You can show me your wine collection."

He didn't need to rest. His hard-on proved that, but he wanted to share his wine collection with Aubrey. No one but his grandfather knew the extent of his interest in enology. He laced his fingers through hers, led her back to the kitchen and folded back the wooden cabinet doors concealing his built-in wine refrigerator.

Her eyebrows lifted. How he managed to keep his eyes on her face when her luscious naked body was there to tempt him he didn't know. "You're a serious collector."

"I have more."

"Show me."

But instead of taking her to the cases stored in the third bedroom he led her to the library. She released his hand and strolled toward the ceiling-high bookcases. The shift of her buttocks and the swish of her long legs as she crossed the room, followed by the sight of her fingers caressing the spines of his collection of books on enology and viticulture, had him gritting his teeth on a surge of pure, unadulterated lust.

"My family has an estate in Napa. It belonged to my grandparents. Maybe you and I…" Her voice trailed off. Regret darkened her eyes and turned down the corners of her luscious mouth. They couldn't visit her family's estate without word of their affair getting out.

She sank in his leather desk chair, tucked her knees to her chest and spun the chair around. Butter-soft ivory skin on burgundy leather. Liam's fingers flexed in anticipation. If he had a condom with him he'd have her flat on her back on top of his cherry desk in seconds. He considered making a quick trip to his bedroom to retrieve protection, but a knock at his front door doused his desire like a coach's sideline shower from the water cooler after a ball game.

Aubrey planted her feet on the floor and halted the chair with a jerk. Her eyes widened with alarm and her face paled. "Are you expecting someone?"

"No." Liam tried to think but it wasn't easy with a naked lady sitting in his desk chair. "It's probably Cade. Otherwise the doorman would have called."

"Cade's a friend?"

"And a co-worker."

"Oh." A dose of apprehension flavored the word.

"Head for my room. I'll get the door."

"You might want to put on some pants first in case it's not your friend."

Where was his brain? Lost somewhere between Panic Avenue and Lust Lane. "Good idea."

The knocking continued as they raced back to Liam's room. He yanked on his pants and then closed the bedroom door on his way out. "All right. I'm coming."

He paused a second to catch his breath and then opened the door. Cade stood on the threshold. His friend immediately stepped inside, heading for the den, the way he had dozens of times before.

"I was about to give up on you. Mind if I hang out here for a while? Jessie and her girlfriends are *oohing* and *aahing* over wedding magazines. They kicked me out." When Liam remained by the door instead of following him, Cade turned and took in Liam's bare chest, the pants he'd fastened but hadn't bothered to belt and his bare feet. "Did I get you out of bed?"

Liam wiped a hand over his face and shut the door. It was pretty damned obvious from his state of undress that Cade had interrupted something. Better his buddy think he'd awakened him than have him ask questions. "Yes."

And the lie began. At that moment it hit home exactly what a relationship with Aubrey would entail. Sneaking around, lying to family and friends and keeping quiet about the only woman who'd put a smile on his face since Patrick's contest began.

Cade's gaze drifted past Liam to the champagne, roses and purse still on the dining room table. "You're not alone."

Damn. You couldn't lie with two empty champagne flutes in plain view. "No."

Cade pointed at Liam's neck. "Is that what I think it is?"

"What?"

"A hickey."

Liam fought the urge to cover his heating skin. "Possibly."

A wicked grin spread over Cade's face. "If you'd mentioned you had a hot date tonight I wouldn't have dropped in. So who is she?"

"Nobody you know."

"The gallery lady with you in the picture in the paper?"

"Good night, Cade. We'll hang out another time."

"You're not talking? She must be special."

Denial sprang to Liam's lips, but he bit it back. Aubrey special? She was, but not in the way Cade meant. There wouldn't be a wedding at the end of this affair. Liam opened the door, an unsubtle hint. "I'll catch up with you Monday."

"I knew you were having women troubles," Cade said on his way past. "You've been zoned out all week. But I guess you've worked them out."

Not good to know his distraction was obvious. "No troubles to work out."

But he lied. Liam shut the door and leaned against it. The trouble had just begun. He'd chosen a path through a mine field. One misstep and life as he knew it could be blown to hell.

What if they'd been caught?

Aubrey's heart beat a frantic *baboom* as she pulled on her clothing. With her hands trembling like fall leaves in a stiff breeze, rolling up the expensive stockings was beyond her capabilities. She wadded them up and stepped barefoot into her heels.

The low rumble of male voices carried through the door, but she couldn't understand the words. No matter. As soon as Liam's visitor left she had to go. Spending the night and brazenly waltzing outside in the morning sunshine was too risky. Better to slink home under the cover of darkness.

A clandestine affair. So over the top. So Hollywood. So not her. And yet she wasn't ready to give up Liam. Not yet. Not when she finally felt alive again for the first time in years.

The opening bedroom door startled her. She spun to face Liam. His gaze ran over her and a pleat formed between his eyebrows. "You're dressed."

"Yes. I need to go."

"Why?"

"Because staying isn't a good idea. I thought— But no. I mean I—" She was blathering. She stopped and pressed her fingers to her lips.

He cupped her shoulders. "Aubrey, it's okay. No one knows you're here."

She looked into his understanding blue eyes and almost caved. Almost. She'd love to spend the night pleasuring Liam and letting him return the favor, because he was exceptionally good at delivering pleasure, and she'd love to wake up in arms, but the stakes were too high. "I want to go home."

"Spend the weekend with me. We'll drive to the coast or upstate and find a place where we don't have to worry about anyone knocking on our door." His thumbs stroked the hollows beneath her collarbones with thought-blocking sensuality.

"I can't. My father is entertaining tomorrow night. I'm his hostess. Maybe next weekend."

He shook his head. "Next weekend I have to fly to Colorado for Cade's engagement party."

Aubrey sighed in resignation. Their time together would consist of stolen interludes, until finding time for each other became more hassle than happiness and one or the other of them would end the relationship. Had she expected otherwise? No, because she hadn't bothered to think that far in advance. In fact, thinking seemed to be an ability she lacked around Liam Elliott.

The relationship was moving too fast. Aubrey needed to step back and assess the situation. Otherwise, she'd end up in one of her mother's relationship train wrecks.

"I want to go home," she repeated.

He must have recognized the determination in her eyes, because he didn't argue this time. He raked a hand over his hair, standing the blond strands up in spikes. "I'll call a cab."

"No. It's only a few blocks."

"Then I'll walk you to your door."

"No." She bit her lip. She hadn't intended to shout.

His lips flattened. "Either I walk you to your door or you take a cab. It's better to risk exposure than have you get mugged or worse."

Once again, his thoughtfulness surprised her. Liam Elliott was truly a prize. A prize she couldn't keep.

"You can walk me to the street corner in view of the well-lit entrance to my building, but not to my door." If she wanted to protect her heart, then she had to keep the boundaries of this affair firmly in sight.

Liam's week had been a tug-of-war between family duty, his friendship with Cade and his desire for Aubrey. There had been moments where it seemed like he—the rope—would snap.

He'd spent his days at work, dodging Cade's knowing smirk and probing questions, trying to pacify antsy advertisers and attempting to alleviate the tension between the EPH staff members. Each evening he came home to Aubrey. She made the headaches disappear. He cooked dinner with her and had the hottest sex of his life. And they talked. About anything, about nothing. It didn't matter. Just being with her was enough.

He couldn't leave town without saying goodbye. Again. They'd said goodbye last night very satisfactorily. If he was a little worried that he was becoming too dependent on her, then he shrugged it off as a temporary hurdle. All too soon this sensual interval would end.

Hoping Aubrey wouldn't mind being awakened so early in the morning, he snatched up his cell phone and punched in her number. He'd programmed her as number one on his speed dial list. He tucked the unit beneath his ear and resumed shoving clothing and his toiletry bag into his suitcase.

"Hello," Aubrey answered in a sleep-roughened voice.

One word, that was all it took to reignite the sparks of hunger deep in his belly. "I called to say goodbye before I take off for the airport."

"It's only five-thirty. You're getting an early start."

He didn't want to go. The realization surprised him. He'd always wanted to travel, but he'd stayed close to EPH, fearing that if he left he'd give the impression that he didn't care about his job. In other circumstances he'd love to see Colorado and spend time with his family away from the stress of work, but the timing of Cade's engagement party reeked. Liam loved Cade like a brother and he was happy his friend had found Jessie, but watching the lovers cuddle and kiss would rub salt in an open wound. Liam and Aubrey could never have what Cade and Jessie had—an open relationship and a family celebration.

Did he want that?

"Liam?"

"I'm here. I was just recalling dinner last night."

"We never got around to eating last night, if you recall."

He grinned. "I feasted, if *you* recall."

Husky laughter filled his ear. "I vaguely remember you nibbling somewhere."

He'd done more than nibble. He'd sipped from her sweetness right there on the dining room table until she begged him to stop, and then he'd carried her to bed because she'd claimed her legs were too weak to support her. Once there she'd made him a very, very happy man.

He'd miss her, he realized. He'd miss her sassy, irreverent humor, her calming voice, her sexier-than-sin body and her amazingly talented mouth. He started to tell her and then clamped his jaw shut on the words. Their relationship rules didn't permit those kinds of declarations. No mention of the future allowed. All they had was here and now.

And that didn't bother him. Much.

"I'll call you from Colorado if I get a chance. If not, you'll hear from me when I get back. Are we still on for Sunday night?"

"I'll be there with bells on—and nothing else."

He groaned at the provocative image.

"Liam, I…I'll miss our evenings together."

His heart thumped hard against his ribs. "Me, too."

"Have fun."

"I'll try." And he would try because duty to his friend and his family demanded he give one hundred percent. And Liam always did his duty.

Seven

Pitiful, you can't even make it twenty-four hours without talking to Aubrey.

Liam itched to share everything he'd seen on Travis Clayton's ranch with her. The place was far beyond Liam's experience. He felt like a wide-eyed kid. Whichever way he turned new sights, sounds and smells inundated him. The air was clean. His lungs would appreciate a morning run here without the exhaust fumes to choke him. And he couldn't get over the lack of noise. Sure, cattle did whatever cattle do, and there were other ranch sounds, but the constant drone of noise to which he'd become accustomed was missing.

He escaped the family gathering in Silver Moon Ranch's large, two-story log house as soon as possible and found a spot in the shadows of the bunkhouse where even the moonlight didn't penetrate. He hit speed dial and Aubrey's number dialed automatically. She answered on the first ring and his pulse did its usual stutter upon hearing her voice.

"You won't believe this place," he blurted without preamble. "The ranch is so vast I can't see anything for miles, but the view of the Rocky Mountains is incredible."

"Hello to you, too," she teased. "You've never traveled west?"

"Other than L.A. and Dallas a few times on business, no. I'm a city boy, born and bred. Would you believe Cade, Shane and I are staying in an actual bunkhouse with two of the ranch hands? It's like walking onto a Western movie set."

"Your uncle Shane?"

"Yeah." Though only a few years older than Liam, Shane was his uncle, and the editor in chief of *The Buzz* magazine.

"Is the rest of the family at the ranch with you?"

The family. Family she'd never meet. The knowledge dampened his mood.

"It's primarily the *Charisma* staff," he responded. "Besides Cade and Jessie, his fiancée, there's Aunt Fin, Jessie's birth mother, my grandmother Maeve, my cousin Scarlet and her fiancé John Harlan."

"John Harlan from Suskind, Engle and Harlan advertising agency?"

"Yes. You know him?"

"Yes. He's handled a few of our advertisers' accounts and attended several Holt Enterprises receptions."

Liam's neck prickled in warning. But there was no reason for Aubrey's name to come up and no reason for John to make the connection between Liam and his forbidden lover. Liam dismissed his concerns.

"Tomorrow's the big day. Jessie's father Travis says neighbors will drive in from all over the state for Cade and Jessie's engagement party. It sounds like he has some interesting entertainment lined up for us city slickers."

She laughed. "Don't hurt yourself. I need you fully functional when you return because I went shopping today. You're going to love what I bought."

He groaned, recalling the last bagful of sinful lingerie she'd sprung on him. Her little fashion show and the resulting action between the sheets had made them both late returning to work from the lunch break they'd taken at his apartment Wednesday.

"I can't wait." His voice sounded as if someone had poured a load of gravel down his throat.

How did she do it? How did Aubrey Holt get to him through a phone line? Until Aubrey, Liam had never been one to spend a great deal of time talking on the phone unless the call was business-related. A phone was a tool. She'd turned it into an instrument of seduction. He found himself reluctant to say goodbye. "What are you wearing?"

"Bubbles. I'm in the tub."

The blood drained from his head. He leaned back, resting his head and shoulders against the rough siding of the bunkhouse. It took a few seconds to get his tongue to work. "You fight dirty."

She chuckled. "So you always claim. But you love it. Otherwise you wouldn't have a smile on your face each time you accuse me of it. I'll bet you're smiling now."

She knew him too well. How had that happened in less than three weeks? He tried to erase his grin and failed miserably. "What man wouldn't smile when he's talking to a sexy naked lady who looks good, smells good and tastes even better?"

"*Someone,*" she continued in a sassy tone, "gave me a bag of steamy romances to read, and the tub is my favorite reading spot. I expect to spend quite a bit of time here while you're gone."

An image of her slender curves, glistening wet and dotted with soap bubbles, flashed in his brain. His mouth filled with moisture, and need twisted in his belly. "You're killing me, sweetheart."

The crunch of a shoe on the hard-packed dirt made him turn. Cade stood only a few feet away in a pool of moonlight.

"I have to go. Good night." Liam barely waited for Aubrey's reply before he snapped his phone closed.

Cade leaned against the corner of the bunkhouse. "I wondered where you'd run off to. I didn't know you needed to whisper sweet nothings to your lady."

Liam didn't know how much his friend had heard, but clearly, denial would be pointless. He replayed as much of the conversation as he remembered. Had he called Aubrey by name? He didn't think so. "Did I miss anything?"

"Travis is getting ready to open the champagne you brought." He pushed off the building as Liam reached his side. "Still not willing to reveal who the mystery lover is?"

"Does it really matter? You don't know her." Liam headed for the ranch house.

"I spilled my guts to you. The least you can do is return the favor."

"No need. My 'guts' aren't going to be dragged down the aisle."

And for the first time, Liam realized that might not be a good thing.

Done. Aubrey shut down her computer, satisfied that the e-mail version of the report on EPH from the advertising staff had been deleted and the paper copy shredded. Her father would have to find someone else to do his dirty work.

"What brings you in on the weekend?" Speak of the devil. Her father stood in the doorway of her office.

She swallowed to ease the sudden dryness of her mouth. "Nothing special. I often work on weekends."

"With the way you've been bolting out the door each day exactly at five, I imagine you have some catching up to do."

She fought a flinch. Evidently, her comings and goings hadn't gone as unnoticed as she'd hoped. "I'm trying to add an evening workout to my schedule."

The lie rolled easily off her tongue. Too easily considering she never lied. But then Liam made certain she had a thorough workout each evening—just not the kind she implied to her father. She hoped the warmth of her cheeks didn't give her carnal thoughts away.

"You've had several lunch meetings this week. With whom?"

Anger stirred. Her father's tendency to micromanage shouldn't extend to her lunch hours. "Friends. I've been working so hard lately that I've lost touch with quite a few of my college friends, and I've only been out twice."

Another lie…sort of. She had lost touch with her friends, but on those lunch hours she'd met Liam, not her former dorm mates.

"Make sure your reunions don't interfere with your work."

"Yes, sir. Absolutely." The urge to stand and salute almost overwhelmed her.

He left as abruptly as he'd arrived without the courtesy of a goodbye. Aubrey sighed. Some things never changed.

Matthew Holt never said hello.

He never said goodbye.

He never said he loved her.

She'd willingly give up a lifetime of hellos and goodbyes just to hear those three words from her father's lips one time.

City meets country. Liam studied the crowd. He didn't have to be related to any of the guests to distinguish Travis Clayton's rural denim-clad neighbors from the New York crowd. Even their casual wear shouted urban.

"Great party, Travis," Liam said as he accepted a draft beer from Jessie's father. Big and blond and gruff, the man clearly doted on his only daughter. The open affection wasn't something Liam had seen often from his own father until lately. His mother's cancer had reaffirmed the value of family connections for all of them.

"I hope you're enjoying yourself."

"I am." As were the rest of his family. Liam's gaze drifted from his host to the crowd scattered across the yard of the Silver Moon Ranch. His grandmother, Cade and Jessie had gathered with several other guests near one of the bonfires scattered about the yard to ward off the October chill. While it was comfortable outside now, Liam had been warned that once the sun set the temperature would drop dramatically.

Aunt Fin stood with a group of locals on the opposite side of the clearing. Fin kept sneaking glances at Travis through eyes the exact shade of green as Jessie's. Now that Liam knew to look for it, the resemblance between Jessie and Fin was remarkable. How Jessie had hidden in plain sight as *Charisma's* intern and not been recognized as Fin's long-lost daughter remained a mystery. Cade had suspected Jessie of having secrets. No one had expected the secret to be that she'd joined EPH to meet the woman who'd given her up for adoption twenty-three years ago. The reunion between mother and daughter had been a happy one.

Liam spotted Shane chatting up a buxom blonde and smiled. Typical Shane. Liam's gaze moved on to John Harlan emptying his pockets onto a nearby table as he prepared to join the short line of guests waiting to mount the "bull," a barrel suspended between two trees. Liam's cousin Scarlet stood nearby, calling encouragement to her fiancé.

"Ready for a turn on the bull?" Travis asked.

"Why not? Giving you a good laugh is the least I owe you for your hospitality."

"I promise not to laugh too hard when you eat dirt." And then Travis turned to look in Fin's direction. Did his aunt and Jessie's dad have the hots for each other? Liam wished Travis luck. Fin was as dedicated to her job as Liam was to his, maybe more so.

Liam shook his head. Only a guy drowning in insatiable lust would recognize the symptoms in another man. The old adage "misery loves company" seemed apt. But in twenty-four hours his misery would be over. He'd be back home with Aubrey.

He headed across the yard toward the barrel and joined the short line of other men foolish enough to risk injuring themselves with the cowboy-style entertainment provided by their host. Liam set his beer on the table, emptied his pockets and laid his cell phone beside Travis's other guests' belongings. Leaving his wallet out in the open was definitely not a risk Liam would have taken in the city, but here it seemed as acceptable as leaving the bunkhouse door unlocked last night.

Liam's family members gathered to watch him, as if the possibility of him sustaining bodily harm interested them. He rested an arm across his grandmother's shoulders. "If I break my neck will you scatter my ashes on the beach at The Tides?"

"Ooh, hush with your teasing. And be careful, will ya, love?" she scolded him in the soft Irish brogue she hadn't lost in more than fifty years of living in the States. She turned to Fin, who'd sidled up between Cade and Jessie. "Why is it boys have to prove their manhood long after they've started shaving?"

"Good question, Mother," Fin replied.

Liam intercepted another one of those heated glances between his host and his aunt. *Interesting.*

John stayed on the "bull" a respectable amount of time

before falling into the deep pile of wood shavings below. The guy in line in front of Liam, one of Travis's ranch hands, climbed on board. The cowboy made riding the pitching barrel look easy. Everyone stopped to watch until he jumped off.

Travis clapped Liam on the back. "Climb on, Elliott. Let's see what you're made of."

Liam hoped he didn't embarrass himself. "How long did John last?"

"Seven seconds," the guy with the stopwatch called out.

Seven seconds. Liam psyched himself up. He could handle seven seconds. The ranch hands held the barrel steady as Liam swung his leg over the top. The cowhide blanketing the metal slipped and he nearly went over the side. Finally, he found his balance, tucked his heels under as instructed, grabbed the rope handle with his right hand and raised his left arm in the air. "Let's go."

The cowboys working the ropes to give the "bull" its motion yanked. Liam fought for balance. Riding the barrel reminded him of piloting the small Sunfish sailboat they kept at The Tides in rough seas. The barrel pitched and bucked, rose and dropped.

"Who has Aubrey Holt as number one on speed dial? I picked up your cell phone by mistake," John called out.

Oh, hell. Liam tried and failed to regain his balance. He hit the ground with a thud. The impact winded him. He shoved to his feet, brushing sawdust from his jeans and sweater. "Mine," he wheezed. "It's my phone."

"*Aubrey Holt* is your mystery lover?" Cade asked, his tone one of disbelief.

A quick scan of his family's faces revealed the same shocked expressions on each one. Denial sprang to Liam's lips, but he didn't voice it. Affirmation would set loose an unpleasant chain of events, but he couldn't cheapen the peace, pleasure and happiness Aubrey had brought him by lying. "Yes."

John stepped forward, offering Liam his phone. "I'm sorry. Yours is the same model as mine and it was next to my wallet on the table. I picked it up by mistake. When I tried to make a call using speed dial I reached the wrong number. I checked the name on the screen and saw Aubrey's. You might want to call her and explain."

As a partner in an advertising agency, John would be aware of the rivalry between Holt Enterprises and EPH. He'd understand the repercussions of the hornet's nest he'd just disturbed. But Liam couldn't blame him. "An honest mistake, John. No problem."

The compassion in John's eyes said he knew Liam lied.

In a matter of minutes someone would call Patrick Elliott and tell him that his grandson was consorting with the enemy's daughter, and Liam's problems would begin in earnest. He needed to call Aubrey and warn her that this could be the beginning of the end of their relationship.

His fingers tightened around the phone. He wasn't ready to let go of her yet, but without a doubt he'd have to say goodbye to Aubrey all too soon.

Over. The most exciting romance of her life would soon be over.

Aubrey paced Liam's apartment Sunday evening feeling slightly sick to her stomach. Liam would be home soon. She'd known from the moment he called last night to tell her their affair had become public knowledge that she'd broken her promise to herself to keep her heart and hormones separate. Liam had become too important to her. Their meetings had become the highlight of her days—not just for the sex, which was amazing, but for his friendship, the shared dinners, the conversation and the understanding she saw in his eyes when she talked about her frustration with her job.

She didn't want to lose the man who'd given her something besides work to look forward to for the first time in seven years. But what choice did she have? Liam would never choose their temporary fling—no matter how satisfying or incendiary—over his family.

Thursday night he'd given her keys to his apartment so that she could be waiting for him when he returned. He'd want them back. He'd tell her goodbye. And according to the rules they'd established that would be it. No begging for more time. No clinging. She wasn't sure she could say goodbye gracefully, with dignity.

Even if Liam was willing to risk Patrick Elliott's wrath to keep her in his life, she'd have to face the same dilemma. Maintaining her relationship with Liam meant displeasing her father. Again. It was only a matter of time before her father had enough of her disappointments and wrote her off as an employee, as a daughter. And did she really want to burn her bridges over something as temporary as an affair?

The feelings in her heart didn't feel temporary. But they were. She knew it just as well as she knew her mother would fall in love and marry again once she got over the most recent heartbreak with husband number five.

The sound of a key grating in the lock sent her heart plunging to her stomach. The door opened and Liam stood on the threshold with his suitcase in hand. Somber blue eyes met hers. Aubrey couldn't have spoken if her life depended on it. Emotion welled in her throat, blocking all sound. What was he thinking? How to say goodbye? How to tell her to get out?

"You're here." His voice was low and flat, as devoid of emotion as his face.

"Yes. I—" She dampened her lips and swallowed. "I said I would be."

Liam stepped inside and closed the door. He dropped his bag and his coat in the foyer. Without a word he crossed the room, captured her face in his palms and kissed her.

She didn't know what she'd expected, but this deep, soul-robbing kiss wasn't it. Liam devoured her mouth like a starving man would his first meal after breaking his fast, ravishing her with teeth and tongue and lips. His kiss was a little wild, a little rough and a whole lot sexy. His fingers raked through her hair, over her shoulders, down her back, and then back again. He systematically removed her clothing. Blouse. Bra. Shoes. Slacks. Panties. She stood in front of him naked, quivering and confused.

Liam kicked off his shoes and within a minute his garments lay piled on top of hers on the floor. He barely gave her time to admire the ripple of muscles beneath his skin before tumbling her onto the sofa. His hands moved swiftly, painting a trail of goose bumps over her skin, stealing her breath and her sanity and stirring a vortex of need deep inside her. He sipped and nipped from her neck to her navel and then lower. She fisted her hands in his short hair, bowing her back, lifting her hips toward his mouth and the magic he created. She crested swiftly—too swiftly—giving her no time to question his silent desperation.

He grabbed his pants, retrieved his wallet and protection, which he quickly donned. And then he knelt between her legs, cupped her bottom and filled her. He pumped deep, fast, relentlessly pounding her toward the edge of reason. He didn't try to hold back or sustain her pleasure the way he usually did. This time he raced for fulfillment as if he were afraid it would escape him, and Aubrey greedily accepted everything he gave. If anything, she urged him on, stoking his broad shoulders, kneading his tight butt, lifting her hips for each plunge.

Tension coiled tighter inside her and her lungs labored as if she raced with him, and then waves of ecstasy crashed over her. She dug her nails into his biceps and studied his face, trying to memorize the moment as Liam groaned and arched in climax. For seconds they stayed frozen, bodies locked together, gazes connected.

His eyes said it all. The end. Tonight would be their last night. And then he collapsed to his elbows, resting his forehead beside hers on the sofa cushion. That this would be their final coupling brought tears to Aubrey's eyes. They seeped into her hair. Not wanting Liam to see her emotional reaction, she hid her face in his shoulder.

Pain squeezed her chest and she could barely choke back her sobs. She'd repeated her mother's mistake of falling in love at first sight. Aubrey looked back on her mother's roller-coaster life with a flash of clarity. Suddenly, she understood the rush and exuberance of the highs and the crushing agony of knowing rock bottom waited just around the corner.

She'd broken the rules and fallen in love with Liam Elliot—the one man she could never have.

"Good morning, Liam," Ann, Liam's administrative assistant, said as he approached her desk. "Your grandfather would like to see you immediately."

Liam's Monday had started out lousy from the moment he'd awakened to the empty pillow beside him—empty except for the keys he'd given Aubrey resting where her head should have been. Apparently, his day was about to get worse.

"Good morning, Ann. Tell Patrick I'll be there in fifteen minutes."

Ann hesitated, her eyebrows arching in surprise. In the past when Patrick cracked the whip Liam had always jumped to do his bidding. Instantly. Without question. Without even going into his own office first.

Not today. Not when Liam hadn't come to terms with Aubrey sneaking out of his apartment in the middle of the night. Not when he didn't know if he could abide by their agreement and make no further contact with her. They'd made love on his couch, in his shower and in his bed last night, and then she'd left while he slept, without saying goodbye.

He wanted an explanation, damn it. How could she walk away from what they had?

"Your messages are on your desk," Ann said, breaking into his thoughts.

"Thank you." He entered his office, closed the door and then took a seat behind his desk. He robotically sifted through the pink message slips without focusing on them and finally shoved them aside and reached for the phone.

No calls at work. The relationship rule stilled his hand.

What if he wasn't ready to let Aubrey go?

What if he still needed her?

Needed her?

Yes, needed her.

He parked his elbows on his desk and rested his head in his hands. What now? Seeing Aubrey openly would cause problems for both of them. But she didn't like her job. Maybe he could convince her to quit. Patrick would never give her a job here, but there were other publishers in Manhattan—publishers Patrick didn't despise.

Liam's office door flew open. Patrick stormed in without bothering to knock. "How dare you consort with the enemy's daughter."

And the battle began. Resigned, Liam sat back in his chair.

"Holt Enterprises isn't the enemy. It's the competition. One of many publishers in the magazine market."

"Holt isn't like our other competitors. He uses underhanded tactics to get what he wants. What makes you so sure that Aubrey Holt isn't pumping you for information?"

"Because we don't discuss business." Other than in the most general sense of work frustrations. He hadn't told her about Patrick's insane method of choosing a successor. But he'd come close a few times. He needed to discuss the chaos with someone. Someone not caught up in the rivalry tearing EPH apart.

"Not good enough. End it," his grandfather ordered.

Maybe he should, but he couldn't. Not yet. Not when he still ached for her and she occupied his thoughts 24/7.

During the weekend in Colorado the story of how his grandfather had bullied Aunt Fin into giving up her baby twenty-three years ago had been repeated numerous times for Travis's guests. Fin had spoken openly of the pain, regret and anger that had followed—anger that even now strained her relationship with her parents, Maeve and Patrick.

Patrick wasn't always right. He wasn't right now.

"Whether or not I continue to see Aubrey is none of your business."

"I'm making it mine. You work for me and what you do reflects on EPH. End it with Holt's daughter or else—"

Liam rose sharply and leaned forward, bracing his arms on his desk. "Patrick, do you really want to issue that ultimatum? Because at this moment, after the year of hell you've put us—the company and the family—through, you have no guarantee that I won't walk."

The blue eyes so similar to the ones Liam saw in the mirror each morning hardened and then filled with something else. Resignation? Liam wasn't sure. "Then I suggest you take some time off until you know where your loyalties lie."

Liam's stomach clenched. "Are you ordering me out of the office?"

"Until you're ready to end your association with Aubrey Holt I don't want you in this building."

So this was it. Time to choose between family duty and his own happiness. It should have been an easy decision. But it wasn't. In fact, last night he'd intended to tell Aubrey goodbye, but he hadn't been able to say the words or let her go. For the first time Liam wanted to be selfish and put his needs above the family's, above EPH's. And for the first time, he just might.

"You don't trust me to keep my business and personal life separate?"

Patrick's mouth flattened. "It's not a risk I'm willing to take."

"Fine. I'm out of here." But he wasn't leaving without saying what had been eating at him since January. "You might want to keep in mind that *you* are the one who betrayed me, Patrick. You used what I told you in confidence about members of this family to pit them against each other with your idiotic challenge. You are solely responsible for the self-destruction of EPH."

"I'm busy, Aubrey. What is it that can't wait?" Matthew Holt asked without looking up from papers in front of him.

Aubrey stood in front of his desk, knotting her fingers, battling nerves and bracing herself for the worst. She'd decided confronting her father immediately would be better than the torture of worrying he'd uncover her secret and attack her unexpectedly.

"I've been seeing Liam Elliott."

His expression darkened and he abandoned his work. She had his full attention now. "You've what?"

"I've been dating Liam Elliott. I wanted to tell you before you heard it from someone else."

"Stop seeing him."

Very likely a moot point, but not her father's decision to make. "I'm twenty-nine, too old for you to choose my boy-friends, Dad. I'll decide when and if to end a relationship."

His steely-eyed stare had caused her capitulation too many times to count, but not this time. Aubrey held his gaze, refusing to concede.

"Are you sleeping with him?"

She recoiled from the invasive question. Her father had never been one to offer personal advice. That had fallen to Jane, his personal assistant. But the fire in her cheeks had probably already given him his answer. "Yes."

"I asked you to get information out of him, not screw him. Is that what you're doing? Using pillow talk to get what you need?"

It would be so easy to lie, to tell him what he wanted to hear and maybe, just maybe, see respect in his eyes for once. But she didn't condone her father's methods and she wouldn't pretend she did. "Liam and I don't discuss work, and I would never use or deceive him that way."

He rocked back in his chair and studied her through narrowed eyes. "You're in love with him."

The comment—more of an accusation, really—startled her because once again, it wasn't a territory father and daughter had ever covered.

"Yes." For now. But who knew how long this heady feeling would last?

He tapped his pen on his desk for twenty-two agonizing beats. Aubrey knew because she counted—anything to keep her mind off her churning stomach.

"I want you to be happy, Aubrey, and if Elliott makes you happy…" He shrugged. "But if any confidential information leaks from Holt Enterprises and I even suspect it came from you, then you will be fired. Is that clear?"

"Yes, sir." What was clear was that her father would put business before his daughter. No surprise there.

"What have you found out about the EPH situation?"

Liam had referred to "Patrick's stupid competition" on more than one occasion, but she'd share neither the sales department report nor anything else that could hurt Liam with her father. "Nothing."

"Then start digging." He dismissed her by turning back to his paperwork. Discussion over.

Telling him she wouldn't be his spy would be a waste of breath. Besides, she'd probably never see Liam again. She'd ended the relationship by leaving his keys behind, and they'd promised no further contact if either one of them walked away.

Walking out of his apartment this morning had been one of the hardest things she'd ever done. She assured herself the ache in her chest was temporary. Her mother had always recovered from her broken hearts and Aubrey would too, eventually. But it certainly didn't feel like it at the moment. At the moment it felt as if someone had extinguished the sun.

She returned to her office. A courier stood in front of Linda's desk. "There she is," her administrative assistant said. "Aubrey, he has a package for you that only you can sign for."

Aubrey signed the electronic box and accepted the flat envelope. Curious, she checked the return address.

Ernie's Pub. Liam's favorite lunch spot.

Her stomach dropped and her heart slammed against her ribs. "Thank you."

She hustled into her office, shut the door and ripped open the envelope. Inside she found an airline ticket with a small piece of notepaper clipped on top.

"Napa Valley's calling. Join me? L." She brushed her trembling fingers over Liam's bold handwriting. He hadn't followed their relationship rules, either.

Adrenaline raced through her veins, flushing her skin and shortening her breath. She collapsed into her chair and pressed her hand to her chest while she examined the ticket more closely. First class to San Francisco, departing at nine tomorrow morning.

Tomorrow.

A wise woman would courier the ticket right back to Liam Elliott with a "Thanks, but no thanks" note and let this temporary fascination with him fade. She should walk away before sustaining further—and possibly permanent—damage to her heart. They didn't—*couldn't*—have a future together. The sooner she quit feeding the habit of seeing him, the sooner her craving for him would fade.

Obviously, graduating magna cum laude wasn't a true reflection of intelligence because Aubrey reached for the intercom button.

"Linda, clear my calendar for the next two weeks. I'm taking some personal time, and I'm not sure how long I'll be gone."

Eight

He was about to give up when he spotted her. Exhilaration flooded Liam as he watched Aubrey cut a path through the tourists and business travelers in the busy terminal. Long, lean, chic and, he'd discovered to his delight, every bit as flexible as she'd promised at their first meeting, Aubrey Holt called all of his senses to attention.

Her hair swirled around her shoulders as she turned her head, scanning the area around the gate, and then her violet gaze collided with his, winding him like a blow to the solar plexus. Her steps faltered and then she continued toward him.

Alarm bells clanged in his subconscious as he rose. He shouldn't be this happy to see her.

Was he falling for her? Falling for his forbidden lover?

Impossible. He knew the relationship was temporary.

But why else would you be stupid enough to risk alien-

ating Patrick, the one man you've spent your entire life trying to please?

Liam stifled his intrusive conscience and met Aubrey at the end of the line in front of the check-in counter. He tightened his grip on his laptop case when what he really wanted to do was grab Aubrey, pull her close and hold her. The scent of summer roses drifted to him. "I'm glad you came."

A tentative smile trembled on her lips. "What made you send the ticket?"

"I wasn't ready to say goodbye. And despite the way you sneaked out, I don't think you are, either."

The tip of her tongue peeked out to dampen her bottom lip. "No. No, I'm not ready. But you broke a rule."

He gave in then to the overwhelming need to touch her, stroking his knuckles across her satiny cheek. He loved the way her pupils expanded and her breath hitched. "I'm trying to be flexible. Like someone else I know."

Laughter sparkled in her eyes, but the airline employee asking for Aubrey's ticket and ID prevented any reply.

"We'll be boarding first class in about twenty minutes," the hostess promised. "Have a good flight."

"Thank you," they said in unison.

He led Aubrey to a seat away from the crowd.

"This trip seems a bit spur of the moment," she offered, filling the silence when he couldn't find words.

How much should he tell her? Should he confess that this trip was a final attempt to get her out of his system? "Patrick kicked me out of EPH until I get my priorities straight."

Sympathy filled her eyes. "I'm sorry."

He covered her hand on the armrest between them, threading his fingers between hers. "Don't be. This isn't your fault. We both knew the risks when we continued seeing each other."

"My father wasn't overjoyed to hear the news, either."

He squeezed her hand. "I decided to take the time to see Napa Valley. I always wanted to go, but work has always seemed more important."

"Where are we staying?"

He shook his head, his mouth twisting wryly. She couldn't possibly know how out of character this trip was for him. He never took off without a firm agenda. "Good question. I made the airline reservations, but I didn't book a hotel. For once in my life I wanted to go with the flow, follow wherever curiosity led me and stop any place that looks interesting. We'll rent a car and drive around. I'd like to tour several wineries, but other than that…" He shrugged. "I'm open to suggestion."

"We could always stay at my grandparents' place. Since our relationship is out in the open we don't have to worry about the household staff reporting back to my father, and the property is centrally located and convenient to almost everything in the valley."

"If the hotels are full I may take you up on that." Wouldn't Patrick love to hear that not only was Liam sleeping with the enemy, he was housed under his roof?

"Does your family know where you're going?"

He hadn't told anyone. Not even Cade. "No. They can reach me by cell phone or e-mail if they need me, but I needed this time for me—for us—before I return to EPH and do what's expected of me."

If he hadn't been looking directly at her, he would have missed her flinch. He hated hurting her, but Aubrey needed to understand that this week would be their last. When it ended he'd go back to his life, his job, his family. His duty.

She smiled, but it did nothing to alleviate the sadness in her eyes. "Then I guess we'd better make the most of our final days together."

* * *

"Ready to admit defeat?" Aubrey asked after the fourth hotel turned them away. Liam had also tried three bed-and-breakfast inns. "It's the tail end of the grape harvest season, Liam, and everything is booked."

"Defeat's not in my vocabulary," he replied as he pulled the car back onto the highway. "How about dinner?"

"Okay. I know a good place." Wind from the open top teased Aubrey's hair, blowing away some of her tiredness. She twisted in the passenger seat of the convertible Liam had rented and studied him. Stubble covered his chin with dark golden spikes, and tiredness dragged his clean-cut features. She'd bet he hadn't slept well after Patrick Elliott kicked him out of the office. Add in an early wake-up and a seven-hour cross-country flight and Liam must be exhausted. She certainly was. An early dinner and bed appealed.

"My grandparents' house is only a few miles down the road. If you're not comfortable staying there for our entire vacation, we can move as soon as we find a hotel room."

Liam shook his head, but kept his eyes on the Route 29 traffic. "I'm supposed to be giving you a romantic vacation, not mooching off your family."

"Oh, I plan to make you pay," she teased him in as sultry a voice as she could manage after a night with too little sleep and a day of too much coffee.

His head briefly swung her way, lingering only long enough for her to glimpse the sexual spark lighting his eyes. "Oh, yeah? How?"

Bittersweet warmth invaded her. This was it. The end. Soon Liam would return to the Elliott fold and she'd be nothing more than a memory. He couldn't possibly know how much hearing his plan had hurt and she'd make sure he never did. She intended to make this a vacation he would never forget, and she hoped that one day soon she'd get past the pain of losing him.

"You'll have to wait and see, but trust me, it involves a lot of sexy lingerie. Turn left here."

The way Liam looked at her when she wore the sinful pieces of satin and lace made her feel womanly and desirable, not flat chested and too tall, so she'd packed accordingly. After this trip she'd probably never wear any of the expensive underwear again. She wouldn't be able to handle the memories attached. She curbed her maudlin thoughts. "I guess you know Napa Valley is the richest agricultural land in the country?"

"Yes, but being here…" He surveyed the surrounding acreage, the neat rows of vines and inhaled deeply. "Seeing the vineyards stretching on either side of the road beats the hell out of reading about it, and you can't smell this in a book."

She laid a hand on his thigh. "You should have come sooner."

"Probably, but I'm glad to be here with you." His fingers laced through hers. How could anything temporary feel this good? She banked the feeling of contentment so that she could pull it out later—after Liam was gone.

"Does anyone in your family know about your interest in winemaking?" They'd left the main highway and heavy traffic behind. She loved the winding back roads, the slower pace.

"Everybody knows I'm interested in wine, but only Patrick has paid any attention to my library and knows my interest goes beyond buying a good-tasting vintage."

"Turn right here. There's a small Italian restaurant ahead. We can eat in or get takeout. Why Patrick? Why not your parents or your brothers or sister?" He'd told her about his family, describing each member so well that Aubrey felt as if she'd already met them. But she wouldn't ever meet them.

"Until Mom's illness Dad was a workaholic. I spent more time with my grandfather than my father. Patrick showed me the ropes of the business. He was the one I went to when I had questions about work, about life."

"So you're close?"

"I thought we were. Now I'm not so sure. You were right about the rumor that he's getting ready to retire. His method for choosing his replacement is—" He flattened his lips and his face filled with frustration. "I don't understand what he's doing and he refuses to explain, but his plan is causing problems at EPH."

"I'm sorry." She didn't want details, because if she didn't know anything then she couldn't feel guilty about not sharing with her father. She hated being torn between the two men she cared most about. "Here's the restaurant."

The stucco building reflected the Spanish-style architecture prevalent in the area. Stucco walls the color of French-vanilla ice cream supported a red clay tile roof. Rounded archways led through an interior courtyard to the restaurant entrance. She didn't come to Napa Valley often, but whenever she did she always stopped here. "It's early and the parking lot isn't crowded. We should be able to get a table if you want to eat here and sample some local wine."

"Sounds good." He climbed from the car, circled it and helped her alight. She clung to his hand and savored the shimmer of awareness skipping up from their parallel palms to settle low in her torso.

"Tomorrow we'll check into visiting the wineries you mentioned." He released her hand to open the door and instantly, she missed the closeness, but then his palm spread over the small of her back. His warmth penetrated her clothing and her skin tingled. Would the day come when his touch didn't affect her as strongly? If she followed her mother's example, Liam would lose impact over time.

He nodded. "Louret and Ashton wineries combined at the beginning of this year to form Kindred Estate Vineyards. I'd like to tour both estates. Louret was a boutique winery that specialized in quality instead of quantity. Ashton produced good wine but in larger quantities. I'm curious to see how the two halves merged into a new whole and if I can still get a case of my favorite Louret Pinot Noir."

"I checked into Louret after you mentioned it the other night because the name sounded familiar. One of our cooking magazines did a story a couple of months ago on Mason Sheppard, their youngest winemaker. I'll call first thing in the morning and see if I can pull some strings to get you a private tour." She turned in his arms and flattened her hands over his chest. "I know you said you wanted to go with the flow, but I'd like to show you some of my favorite parts of the valley. Liam, will you trust me to show you a good time while you're here?"

His eyes glittered with humor but also sensual heat, and suddenly her appetite for food faded and her hunger for Liam increased. "Why do you think I brought you?"

"I meant out of bed as well as in."

"Without a doubt, I trust you, Aubrey."

She touched his cheek, stroking her fingertips over his raspy evening beard and then the softness of his lips. "There are so many things here in the valley that I'd like to share with you."

"I'm all yours, sweetheart."

Oh, how she wished that were true.

The irony of ending the most passionate interlude of her life in the place Aubrey had secretly fantasized about turning into a romantic couples retreat didn't escape her.

"Here we are. Hill Crest House."

Even before she climbed from the car the warmth and the love she'd found here as a child radiated from the two-story colonial's redbrick walls to warm and welcome her. The setting sun cast long shadows over the formal landscaping in front of the house. Her grandfather had insisted on the formality, but Aubrey's favorite place was the rambling garden in the backyard, where her grandmother's love of flowers provided one surprise after the other. As a child Aubrey had spent many hours digging in the dirt alongside Gram, planting flowers, herbs and even a few vegetables.

"Not exactly a grandma's cottage," Liam said beside her.

"No. There are eight bedrooms, each with a private bath, but the house still feels cozy to me, if that makes any sense. I haven't visited in…eighteen months. Time slipped away."

An evening breeze danced over her skin, blowing her hair into her eyes. Liam brushed the strands back with his finger. "You love it here. I can see the tension draining from you."

"Ah, an observant man. No, wait. Isn't that an oxymoron?"

He punished her teasing sarcasm with a quick, hard kiss that tripped her heart. "I'm so observant I noticed lights on in the house."

"The staff would have turned them on before they left at five. Even though the place is only occupied for a few weeks of the year, Daddy keeps a staff year round just in case he decides to fly some associates out."

"Did you notify the staff of our arrival?"

She flashed him an "oh please" look. "Since it took me until halfway through dinner to convince you to accept my hospitality, no. But I'll leave a note in the kitchen so they won't have the local law enforcement officers roust us out of bed in the morning."

"I'll get our bags." Liam extracted their suitcases from

the trunk. Aubrey let him carry the heavier luggage, but grabbed his laptop case and led the way up the brick stairs between the fat, round white columns and onto the covered front porch.

She unlocked the door and stepped inside. *Home.* No, not home. Just her favorite vacation spot. She opened a hinged door concealed by a small painting to access and disarm the alarm system. Liam stopped so close behind her she could feel his heat, inhale his scent even in the vast two-story foyer. She glanced at him over her shoulder and caught a glimpse of the exhaustion on his face before he quickly masked it.

"How about the nickel tour and then we'll take a quick soak in the hot tub before crashing? I know it's early here, but New York time is catching up with me."

"Sounds good."

She indicated the inverted Y-shaped staircase. "Upstairs first. Gram dedicated each suite to one of her favorite plants."

The two branches of stairs joined midair and led to a bridge that connected the east and west bedroom wings of the house. If she faced the front side of the house she overlooked the foyer. The back side of the bridge overlooked the two-story great room below with its massive brick fireplace.

"You can leave the bags here." She indicated the left side of the walkway. "To the right we have the daffodil suite, the wisteria suite and the fern suite."

She indicated each door as they passed. Liam, typical of a man, barely glanced inside. Home decor obviously wasn't his thing. "We also have an elevator and the back stairs on this side of the house."

"An elevator?" The sexy timber of his voice sent a tingle of awareness down her spine.

"Yes."

Mischief sparkled in his eyes. "Christened it yet?"

She struggled to catch her breath as memories pulsed through her. "No."

"Want to?"

Her skin flushed hot all over. "Yes, but not tonight."

"I take it this wasn't a vacation home?" he asked as she backtracked to the opposite side of the house.

"No. My grandparents were older and they'd given up on having children when my dad, a late-in-life surprise baby, arrived. As soon as he was old enough to take over Holt Enterprises my grandparents retired here and left my father in charge."

"They moved halfway across the country and left him to sink or swim in the shark-infested waters of the magazine publishing business?"

"Yes. My grandfather believed experience was the best teacher of all. He always claimed you learned more from failure than success."

"Tough guy."

"Great guy. He taught me that failure wasn't something to fear." The words stalled in Aubrey's brain, a forgotten lesson recalled. She'd been so caught up in trying to please her father since being foisted upon him that she'd forgotten the lessons of her youth.

She shoved the thought back in its hiding place for later examination, retrieved Liam's computer bag from where she'd left it at the top of the stairs and indicated he follow. "This side of the house contains the mint suite, the grape suite and my room, the rose suite."

She led the way into her room and set his computer on the dresser.

"Roses are your favorite flower." It was a statement, not a question.

"Yes. How did you guess?"

He came up behind her, circled her waist with his hands and pulled her against him. She leaned into his warmth, and when he touched his lips to the juncture of her neck and shoulder, she shivered. "Because you always smell like roses."

Aroused despite her long day and restless night, Aubrey turned in his arms, but the pallor of Liam's skin cooled her ardor. She lightly touched her lips to his and then drew back. "Get naked and grab a towel. I'll show you the greenhouse and hot tub. Bathroom's that way."

Liam rolled over in bed, reaching for Aubrey. He found cool sheets instead. Déjà vu. And not a pleasant one, either.

He flopped back on his pillow, surprised at the glitch in his pulse, and he realized his reaction—overreaction—to Aubrey's absence didn't bode well for his plan to say goodbye at the end of the week. His ears picked up the murmur of her voice through the open bedroom door. She was talking to someone somewhere in this huge colonial house. Relief loosened his knotted muscles.

Her voice drew nearer. "Thank you, Mason. That's great. We'll see you tomorrow at eight. Bye."

She walked through the bedroom door with a cordless phone in her hand and the skirt of her burgundy dress swirling around her legs. "Good, you're awake, sleepyhead."

"You're already dressed." He'd awakened with his usual hard-on. Her soft smile and mile-long legs instantly made him harder. He patted the bed and she glided forward and perched on the edge of the mattress.

"My body clock's still on New York time. I have plans for you today." She leaned down and gently nuzzled his lips. "Last night was nice."

Last night after a quick tour of the downstairs and a long

soak in the hot tub they'd fallen into bed exhausted and cuddled until falling asleep. A first for him. He'd never spent the night just holding a woman and surprisingly he'd liked it. Around daybreak Aubrey had awakened him with tender strokes along his spine. He'd rolled over and she'd kissed him softly, which had segued into lazy, slow sex. The gentleness of their lovemaking had blindsided him.

How can you live without that?

Guess you'll find out.

He combed his fingers through her silky hair. "Remind me how nice."

She laughed and pulled away, but a blush painted her cheeks. "Later. Get up and get dressed. I've made reservations for us on the Wine Train. It's a totally touristy thing to do, but fun. We'll begin with a wine tasting at the depot and then lunch during a slow train ride north past twenty-six wineries. In Yountville we'll disembark for a tour of a winery that produces sparkling wine, and then we'll have dessert on the return trip south. Tomorrow you'll get a personally guided tour of both the Louret and Ashton estates from Mason Sheppard. And then on Friday, I'm taking you on a tour of the local brandy distillery. I've never been there, but I've heard you can get drunk from breathing the air."

Aubrey often had that effect on him. Like now, for instance. He threw back the covers, enjoying her gasp at the sight of his erection. "You've been busy. Are you sure we don't have a few minutes?"

She dampened her lips with a slow sweep of her pink tongue and flexed her fingers as if contemplating touching him, tasting him. The need to have those long, slender fingers and those sweet lips on him right now nearly strangled him. But she stepped out of reach before he could drag her deeper into the bed.

"We have to check in by ten-thirty, Liam. Get moving. Breakfast is waiting downstairs."

"Later, then." He rose, cupped her nape and then he kissed her thoroughly, relishing the softness of her lips and the slickness of her tongue. She tasted of cinnamon rolls and coffee. When he lifted his head a flush colored her cheeks, her lips were damp and his heart thumped violently. "Good morning."

Waking up to Aubrey felt good. Too good. But the alarm bells that should have been clanging in his subconscious were suspiciously silent.

Was he in love? Couldn't be. He'd been in love twice in college and both times had been miserable, tense and angst-ridden affairs. He hadn't been able to eat, sleep or study. While Aubrey made him harder than stone on a regular basis, she was also comfortable, exciting and yet restful. He enjoyed being with her, and he didn't have to tiptoe around overly sensitive feelings.

Nah, this wasn't love. It was just a damned good time. Too bad it couldn't last.

"You've done this before?" Liam swiveled his seat on the lounge car of the Wine Train to face Aubrey's.

The only thing better than enjoying her favorite part of California was sharing it with Liam. "Dozens of times. My grandmother took me on my first train ride up the valley when I was six or seven. I try to ride each time I return to Napa, which isn't nearly often enough."

"Then you've seen all this before." His sweeping gesture encompassed the exquisite mahogany paneling, the crystal chandeliers overhead and the vineyards outside the train's windows.

"Not through your eyes. Seeing you soak up every detail of the vintage rail cars and the valley reminds me of a child on Christmas morning. Your enthusiasm is contagious."

He took her hand in his. "Having you around has been an amazing gift."

There he went again, reminding her that this idyllic period would end. Despite the depressing reminder, she realized she hadn't seen Liam this relaxed or happy back in New York. "Have you ever considered leaving EPH?"

His smile vanished. "No."

"Does anyone in your family work outside the company?"

"My cousin Bryan never worked for EPH and several of my relatives, including my sister, have left the company this year." His voice had hardened. "Patrick's selection process is driving them away, and he's too damned stubborn to admit it."

She hated spoiling his mood, and hearing the details of EPH left her conflicted. While she'd like to understand his problems and perhaps help him solve them, knowing meant piling on guilt for not relaying the very information her father had requested.

"Liam, maybe you should consider leaving, too. Estates out here aren't easy to come by because Hollywood types snatch them up in a hurry, but maybe you could find one and try your hand at winemaking. There are more than two hundred wineries in Napa Valley and most of them are privately owned."

"I can't leave EPH."

"Can't or won't?"

"Either. Both. Take your pick."

That looked like yearning in his eyes, but Aubrey decided not to push. When and if Liam was ready to pursue his dream, he'd do so voluntarily. She changed the subject. "I love the area and I have a lot of happy memories of spending time with my grandmother at Hill Crest. My father leases the acreage surrounding the house to another vineyard, so there's always some activity on the property, but the place is peaceful. It's off the main roads, but not so far off that no one can find it. When things get really bad at work, I dream about turning the estate into a bed-and-breakfast."

She bit her lip, not believing she'd just confessed her deepest secret, one she'd not shared with anyone. Liam wasn't the only one who kept secrets from his friends and family.

"Why don't you?" he asked quietly.

"Same old, same old. I owe my father."

"When will that debt be paid?"

His question hit too close to home. Aubrey had begun to believe that no matter what she did it would never be enough for her father. "When will yours? If you're unhappy at EPH, then maybe you should move on."

"Back at you."

"I can't." She hesitated. What did she have to lose by telling the truth? "My father never wanted a daughter. Not before he and my mother divorced and certainly not afterward. When he found out about the incident with my stepfather, I heard him ask his assistant what he was supposed to do with a teenage girl. And then he said, 'If she'd been the son I needed, this wouldn't be a problem.'"

Liam swore, low and succinctly. "So you've what? Been trying to be the son he wanted?"

"I've been trying to be the savvy executive he thinks a son would have been." A sad smile quivered on her lips. "We're a sorry pair, aren't we? Unhappy where we are, but unwilling to make the sacrifices to change our lot."

"Change is…" He shrugged and turned back to the window to study a palatial home as the train passed.

"Scary," she finished for him.

"Risky and selfish. There are too many people to disappoint, including myself."

Liam summed up her feelings well. She didn't want to disappoint her father and she didn't want to disappoint herself by quitting before she proved her worthiness to him.

She wasn't the son he'd wanted. So what? But she was damned good at her job. And she wanted him to notice. Just once. And then she could move on.

Nine

"It's beautiful," Aubrey said from the passenger seat.

Liam, drawn by the wistful tone of her voice, glanced at her as he guided the car down the long driveway. He didn't know whether her comment referred to The Vines, the main house at Louret Vineyards, the steeply roofed two-story winery to the west of the residence or the property as a whole.

"Absolutely breathtaking." He meant her, not the buildings or the land. Would he ever tire of looking at Aubrey, of making love to her, of just plain being with her? What if he didn't? How could he return home and pretend she didn't live just around the corner? But if he didn't, he'd be out of a job.

After yesterday's train ride she'd taken him to another out-of-the-way restaurant for dinner and then surprised him with a charter plane flight over Napa Valley. The pilot had flown the length of the wine country and then circled back over the California coast and the Point Reyes National Seashore on the return trip. Watching the sunset over the Pacific had been spectacular. It was the first time he'd seen the sunset with no skyscrapers to block the view, and he'd watched until the big orange ball sank into the deep blue ocean.

Liam parked the car and, following the signs for the tasting room and store, guided Aubrey across the winery's large porch. He stepped inside and stopped. Like a kid in a candy shop he scanned the bottles lining the walls, searching for his favorites or something new to try.

"May I help you?" asked a woman about Aubrey's height, build and coloring asked from behind a long, high counter. And then she stepped from behind the wine-tasting bar, revealing a heavily pregnant belly.

What would Aubrey look like pregnant? The shocking thought locked Liam's jaws and seized his lungs.

Where had that come from?

Aubrey shot a curious glance his way when he remained mute and then she moved forward, extending her hand. "Hello. I'm Aubrey Holt and this is Liam Elliott. Mason Sheppard is expecting us."

"I'm Jillian Ashton-Bennedict. It's nice to meet you. Your magazine's story on Mason's return to the U.S. was great."

"I'll be sure to pass your compliment on to the writer."

"I'll assist you with the wine tasting after you've finished the Louret half of your tour, because I'm guessing you're not interested in samples at eight in the morning." Her green eyes sparkled with laughter.

Liam found his voice. "No, but we will be later. I have a few Louret favorites, and I'd prefer not to leave without ordering a case or two. Thanks for working us in before your regular tour hours."

"No problem. I'll be happy to help you with your selections when you're ready. Let me call Mason and tell him you're here. He and Darby arrived a few minutes ago." She went behind the counter to use the phone.

He led Aubrey a few yards away to the racks of chardonnay on the wall. "Who's Darby?"

"Darby Quinn, former child actress and now Mason Sheppard's wife. Her story made headlines earlier this year when she and Mason moved back to the States from France."

"I vaguely remember something about that. I'm not into the Hollywood scene."

"I know. You're into sports, finance and wine." Her fingers squeezed his, but her tender smile reached far deeper inside him.

"You think we have it bad in the family lottery. Years ago Darby's mother wrote a tell-all book that painted Darby as a bitch-slash-prima-donna and ruined her acting career. Darby tried to tell the press her side of the story, but no one believed her, especially with her own mother calling her a liar. Eventually, Darby was forced into hiding. And then she literally ran into Mason on a road here in Napa, and she didn't want to hide anymore. She went back to France with him, and while Mason finished his enology studies, they worked together to convince other child stars to come forward and admit that their former manager—who also happened to be Darby's wicked stepfather and former manager—had abused them, too.

"Getting the facts out in the open was a vindication of sorts since Darby had been telling the truth all along. Those she trusted had betrayed her, but the truth set her free by allowing her to return to the States with Mason and to live openly as his wife without the press crucifying her at every turn. Now everyone is speculating about whether she'll return to acting."

Aubrey was a romantic, Liam realized. She had stars in her eyes as she told her fairy tale of a knight coming to a maiden's rescue. He wished he could be Aubrey's knight and rescue her from the job she hated and a father who didn't love her enough.

A big blond guy in jeans and a chambray shirt and a petite blond woman in a vintage-style dress, also noticeably pregnant, came toward them. "Welcome. I'm Mason Sheppard and this is my wife, Darby. Aubrey tells me you're into winemaking."

Liam offered his hand. "Liam Elliott and this is Aubrey Holt. I've read everything I can get my hands on about enology, but I've never tried it."

"Are you thinking of relocating and starting a winery in Napa?" Mason asked.

Darby smiled. "The valley's a great place for new beginnings. I started over here and look what I found."

Merry blue eyes indicated the man at her side and her hand patted her rounded belly. Mason's hand covered hers and the loving look the two exchanged brought a lump to Liam's throat.

Starting over in Napa appealed to him more than it should have. Possibly when he retired... But that day seemed far off. Too far. "One of these days."

With a sweep of his hand Mason indicated the door through which he'd entered. "Let's get started. When we finish here we'll head over to Ashton Estates for a tour of their facility. We've merged Louret and Ashton in many ways under the Kindred Estates umbrella, but because of brand recognition we still carry our old trademarks as well as the new one, and we still have our own production facilities, because frankly we need both to keep up with demand. Aubrey warned me not to hold back on the technical side of the process because she says you're up to it, so if I go too fast or if you have questions, stop me."

Surprised, Liam's gaze found Aubrey's. She'd made sure he received more than the generic spiel offered to tourists. She looked out for him, giving him more than he would have dared hope for. Here and in New York. In bed and out.

Aubrey Holt was perfect for him in so many ways.

He didn't want to let her go.

Ever.

But what choice did he have?

A crushing sensation hit him square in the chest, as if a full wine cask had fallen on him. Liam couldn't breathe, couldn't move, couldn't speak as realization dawned.

He'd fallen in love with the enemy's daughter.

Liam hadn't looked at or touched Aubrey since their tour began almost four hours ago. The absolute silence between them sent a frisson down Aubrey's spine. And the distance. She nibbled her bottom lip in confusion. They stood only a foot apart on the Ashton winery patio, but she might as well have been back in New York.

A tall, dark haired man cradling an infant in a frilly pink romper separated himself from the group gathering on the far side of the patio. Judging by the balloons, flowers and piled gifts Aubrey suspected somebody must be celebrating a birthday.

Mason extended a hand to the newcomer. "Liam and Aubrey, meet my brother-in-law Jared Maxwell. He's married to my half sister, Mercedes, and today is Mercedes's birthday. They're setting up for a surprise party."

Darby took the baby from Jared and snuggled her. "And this cutie pie princess is Chloe. When Jared's not playing Mr. Mom, he runs a string of bed-and-breakfasts in the valley. I take it you have some news of your wife's arrival?" she asked without taking her gaze off the baby.

"Mercedes and Jillian are on their way," Jared replied, keeping a possessive eye on his daughter.

His obvious attachment to the baby gave Aubrey a case of the warm fuzzies. She couldn't recall her father ever looking at her that way, as if his world revolved around her. She swallowed the lump in her throat. "The winery grounds are a perfect setting for a party."

"You should see it on the weekends. The Ashton Estate Winery is a very popular wedding sight." Darby's gaze bounced from Aubrey to Liam and back again, as if she were gauging their interest in a wedding on the grounds. Aubrey's cheeks burned and she looked away.

Darby unexpectedly placed the baby in Aubrey's arms. Startled, Aubrey adjusted her grip. She'd held her friend's children years ago, but there were some things you never forgot, like the warmth of an infant squirming closer, the fresh baby scent or the way a gummy smile and trusting blue eyes could melt your heart. "She's beautiful. How old?"

"Six months," Jared said in a proud voice. His tanned finger trailed across Chloe's downy soft cheek. "And she looks just like her mother."

"If you'll notice, there are a lot of pregnant women and new babies around," Darby said in a teasing tone. "So don't drink the water if a baby's not in your plans."

A tight knot formed in Aubrey's throat. She'd never have Liam's baby. The yearning to hold a child created by their feelings for each other swelled inside her with surprising swiftness.

"I guess I'll stick with the wine, then," she said to fill the awkward silence and then returned the baby to her father.

Liam shifted on his feet beside her. "We should go and let you get on with your party. Mason, Darby, thank you for your time, and thank Jillian for setting up the shipments for me."

Mason shook Liam's hand. "You're welcome, but frankly,

Liam, I enjoyed your visit. Your questions challenged me. You definitely know your stuff. If you ever decide to relocate and set up shop, give me a call. And, Aubrey, if you ever decide to pursue your dream of opening up a B&B, then Jared's the one to guide you. Enjoy the rest of your vacation."

Surprised, Aubrey glanced at Liam. He must have said something to Mason during the tour. "I'll keep that in mind. Thanks. Nice meeting you all."

Aubrey almost had to jog to keep up with Liam on the way back to the rental car. They drove in silence for several miles, and her nerves stretched tighter with each passing moment until finally she couldn't stand it any longer. "Liam, is something wrong?"

He kept his gaze fixed on the road in front of them. "It's a lot to take in."

She couldn't believe the winery information had overloaded him. Aubrey sifted back through the memories of the morning, trying to recall something she or anyone else could have said or done to upset him, and came up empty. The chasm between them had opened before Darby had made her teasing comments about babies and weddings, so that wasn't it.

"Mind if we head back to the house instead of visiting the geyser in Calistoga this afternoon?" he asked.

"Whatever you want. It's your vacation. Old Faithful will still be erupting next time you come to Napa Valley."

The drive to the house took only minutes, but it seemed like hours. The noon sun hung in a blue sky directly overhead, but it couldn't warm Aubrey's chilled skin.

Liam parked, and as they climbed the wide brick front steps, Aubrey stopped him with a hand on his arm. "Did I do something wrong?"

"No. I did." Liam raked a hand through his hair and then

looked at her. What she saw in his eyes stopped her world. "I've fallen in love with you, Aubrey."

So there they were—the words she'd always wanted to hear. Emotions jumbled wildly inside her. Practicality quickly stomped out elation. Judging by Liam's serious expression, he truly believed what he'd said. But this wasn't love. It was lust. He didn't understand the mechanics of tumbling head over heels into love and then falling right back out just as quickly.

And then the doubts crowded in. What if this wasn't one of the short-lived love affairs her mother practiced with regularity and Aubrey let Liam go? No, she had to go with what she knew. This idyllic period would end and she would survive it. Her lips quivered. Her eyes stung.

Before she could speak, Liam's jaw muscles knotted. "But what good is falling in love when a future together is impossible? Part of me wants to walk out and start over here in Napa the way Darby suggested. But I can't, Aubrey. I'm the peacemaker. It's my job to keep Patrick from tearing EPH and the Elliott family apart."

Liam lifted a hand and trailed his knuckles across her cheek. His touch reverberated all the way to her womb. "And I doubt I can convince you to quit your job since you still have things to prove to your father."

He didn't need to add that his grandfather would never accept her into the family fold if she wouldn't quit.

"No, I can't leave Holt Enterprises. Not yet. Maybe never." Her heart swelled, but a cloud of doom overshadowed her joy. She'd known the end was coming, so why did it hurt so much? She captured his hand and held it against her face.

"I love you, too, Liam. But we fell too fast. These feelings won't last. Love like this never does. It's based on physical attraction and not on anything more substantial. Flash-fires burn out as soon as they've consumed the limited fuel supply."

His eyebrows lowered. "Do you honestly believe that?"

"I've seen it happen too many times not to. My mother has fallen instantly and madly in love four times since she left my father. Each time she swore with stars and hope in her eyes that this time it was the real thing, and then a few months or a year later she'd call me. We'd meet for lunch and she'd cry all over me because it hadn't been everlasting love but only another case of lust and infatuation that hadn't last."

His jaw shifted. "And you think that's what this is?"

"I'm afraid so."

What if it's not?

Even if it wasn't, it wouldn't matter. Their duties to their families would keep them apart.

Change her mind or you'll lose her.

Liam stared into the absolute certainty in Aubrey's beautiful violet eyes and knew arguing would be a waste of time. He had to convince her that what she felt for him was more than infatuation.

Lust? There was plenty of that, but his feelings for Aubrey went deeper, and he was damned certain hers for him did too. Hindsight revealed the subtle differences between his college affairs and this. He'd been in lust not love before.

Love meant wanting to give pleasure—in bed and out— and not just take it. Love meant talking, wanting to know his partner's thoughts not just her body. He'd found unbelievable physical pleasure with Aubrey, but he'd also found peace. She thrilled him, but she also soothed him.

Love meant wanting his partner's happiness more than he wanted his own.

Love meant forever, not for however long it lasted.

Lesson one in loving started now. *Give her the time and space she needs to accept what's between them.*

"Then we'd better take advantage of the time we have," he finally replied.

Liam cupped Aubrey's face, brushing her silky hair out of the way and caressing her cheekbones with his thumbs. The pulse at the base of her throat quickened, and his heart kept pace. Her eyes darkened and her lips parted. He wanted to devour her on the front steps of Hill Crest House. Only the knowledge that the staff could see them from the windows reined him in. But a kiss wouldn't hurt. One kiss. One long, slow, seductive kiss.

He sank into the petal softness of her lips, drew in the sweetness of her breath and lost his mind in her taste and in the hot press of her slender curves as she snuggled against him. He mapped her shape with his palms, and then splayed his fingers over her belly. Seeing her face soften as she'd cradled that baby had slammed him with a need to see her holding his child, their child.

But how? How could they make this work?

Her hands mirrored his, stroking, touching. Desire hit him hard and fast, knocking his train of thought off track. Aubrey skimmed her nails beneath the waistband of his slacks and he lifted his head to suck in a sobering breath. The sooner they took this inside the better. Slow wasn't on the agenda this afternoon. He laced his fingers through hers and led her up the brick stairs to the front door.

The flush of arousal pinked her cheeks and her hands trembled as she inserted her key. The door glided noiselessly open on well-oiled hinges. As Liam bent to plant a kiss on Aubrey's nape he spotted a woman—probably a maid he hadn't met yet—disappearing down the upstairs hall toward their bedroom. Maids cleaning upstairs shifted his plans. No bed.

He ducked into the library, towing Aubrey with him, and quietly shut the door. He turned the lock and then leaned against the wood and smiled in anticipation. "What are you wearing under that sexy sundress?"

Her eyes sparkled and her low chuckle teased him like a thousand feathers sweeping over his skin. "You have a lingerie fetish, Liam."

"One you induced. That lace-up top has been making me crazy all morning. Show me what you got, sweetheart." She reached for the ribbon laces, but he brushed her hands aside. "Better yet, let me do a little exploring on my own."

Winding the ends of the laces around his index fingers, he tugged the bow free, and then grommet by grommet he loosened her bodice, revealing one inch of her breast bone at a time. At the halfway point he trailed a finger through the gap.

Aubrey gasped. "There's a zipper in the back. The laces are just for show."

He considered it, but, as much as he wanted to take her hard and fast, slow had its advantages. He wanted to show her with each touch, each kiss how much she meant to him. "Too easy."

And then he lowered his head and pressed a kiss above her neckline over her pounding heart. With his tongue he traced the path his fingers had cleared and with unsteady hands he rapidly loosened the ribbons to her waist to expand his territory.

She wasn't wearing a bra. He eased the halves of her top apart until nothing blocked his view or prevented him from taking a taut raspberry nipple into his mouth. Her fingers dug into his hair, holding him close while he worshipped one breast and then the other. He raked his hands from her waist to her knees, beneath her skirt and back up her thighs until he encountered her smooth bottom. Bare. He explored further, finding a thin strip between her buttocks. Another thong.

Damn. His groin throbbed. Aubrey's sexy underwear would give him a heart attack one of these days. But it'd be worth it.

Hunger screamed through his veins like Fourth of July fireworks as he eased the satin scrap down her legs. She braced her hands on his shoulders and stepped out of the minuscule piece.

Slow down.

He leaned back to look at her, lifting the lingerie to his cheek. "Soft, but not as soft as your skin."

Her nipples were hard and damp, her face flushed and her breathing was as ragged as his. "Before Cade interrupted us at my place, I fantasized about taking you on my desk."

Her gaze darted to the desk in front of the bay window and then back to his face. Her lips parted. "Do it."

"Not worried the gardener might look in?"

"No."

Liam rose slowly. He burrowed his hands beneath her gaping bodice to cup her breasts and thumb the rigid tips. Her eyes fluttered closed and a quiet moan slipped from her lips. He covered her mouth, sipping from her softness until he had to have a taste of her. She tasted like nothing and no one he'd ever had, a flavor uniquely Aubrey's. Addictive. Her tongue met his every stroke, every dip, swirling, tangling, lingering.

Her fingers released the buttons on his cotton shirt and then she ripped the shirttails from his pants and splayed her hands over his pectorals. Her nails combed through his wiry hair with electrifying results. He was so damned hard he hurt. He clasped her waist and pulled her close, brushing his chest over hers, pressing his arousal against her mound and rubbing until he thought the top of his head wouldn't be the only thing to erupt.

Aubrey reached between them to unbuckle and unzip his pants and then she backed toward the desk, shoved a bronze statue and the phone out of the way and hopped onto the glossy surface. She crooked a finger and he gulped. He took one step toward her and then another on unsteady legs.

He loved her. Loved this sassy, confident woman who wasn't afraid to take what she wanted. And she wanted him. The knowledge swelled his heart. He'd make this work. He'd find some way for him and Aubrey to be together.

And then her fingers snagged on the waistband of his boxers, pulling him closer until his thighs bumped the desk top. She shoved the fabric out of the way and her opposite hand curled around his rigid length.

Thinking fell off the priority list. Sensation took over. The smooth stroke of her hand. The inferno of her mouth over his and then on his neck, his collarbone, his nipple. He fumbled for the condoms he now carried in his wallet. His hands shook, but he managed to don protection before pushing her back on the desk, shoving her dress up to her waist and kneeling.

Her heat, scent and moisture filled his mouth, and her cries sounded like music to his ears. He tasted, stroked and laved her until she bowed off the desk and begged him to take her as release after release rolled over her. Even then he stalled, his goal to make her want more than just here and now, to make her want more than fast and furious and out of control. Any man could give her an orgasm. He wanted her to want him. *Him.*

"Liam, please," she whispered. "I need you."

By the time he rose, his knees quaked and Aubrey was a puddle of satisfaction on the desk top.

"Me or just this?" He positioned himself between her legs and bent over her to catch her whimpers with his mouth as he plowed into her slick, tight body. Remaining still in the hot clench of her body made him gasp.

"You. Oh, my… You, Liam. Just you." Aubrey shifted impatiently beneath him.

Her words and wiggles set him on fire. He tried to slow the piston action of his hips, to draw out her pleasure, tried to make himself last beyond her next orgasm, but her hands on his butt, her mouth sipping, nipping and biting, her body squeezing his sent him over the edge far too soon. His hoarse growl of release echoed through the room.

Their labored breaths blended, and their bare chests rose and fell in unison. When the fog cleared from his brain and his lungs no longer burned like fire, he lifted himself an inch or two. He wasn't capable of more.

He met her sexy, satisfied gaze. "I love you, Aubrey. Take as much time as you need to believe this is real. I'll be here."

Worry clouded her eyes and even though she didn't physically pull away and he remained buried to the hilt inside her, he felt the mental distance widen between them. "What if this is love and not just lust—what about our families, our jobs? How can we get around that, Liam?"

"I don't have all the answers yet, but solving problems is what I do best. We'll make this work. You have my word." He caught her chin in his hand. "And, Aubrey, I always keep my promises."

Ten

Ringing jarred Liam from a deep sleep. He blinked open gritty eyes and tried to isolate the sound.

A cell phone. His. He sank back into his pillow. Let voice mail pick up.

Aubrey lay on her stomach beside him with her arm flung over his chest. Naked. Hot. He stroked a hand down her spine and caressed her smooth bottom. Smiling, she purred and snuggled closer. His pulse kicked unevenly as images flashed in his mind of yesterday on the desk and last night on the blanket beneath an apple tree on the backside of the property. Making love with someone you wanted to spend the rest of your life with was a whole different experience.

The ringing stopped. Seconds later it intruded again. Whoever was calling wasn't going to talk to a recording. "Damn."

"You have to answer?" Aubrey mumbled as she rolled to her side, revealing a soft, flushed breast with sheet wrinkles stamped into her pale skin. Once he dealt with the caller he'd trace each crease with his tongue.

"Yes. Where the hell is it?" The last time he'd seen his phone it had been clipped to his belt. They'd undressed at the foot of the bed after returning from the garden and climbed into bed. He threw back the sheet and hunted for his pants under the comforter and spare pillows they'd knocked to the floor. He found his phone buried under her dress and his shirt and snapped it open. "Elliott."

"What in the hell have you done?" Patrick's furious voice bellowed at him.

"Good morning to you, too, Patrick." Liam scraped a hand over his bristly chin and glanced at the clock. Five. Eight, New York time. "What are you talking about?"

"You released confidential financial information to the press."

What? Someone had leaked EPH info? "Wasn't me. I'm on vacation. A vacation you insisted I take, remember?"

"These are *your* files in today's *Times*, Liam, *your* numbers. Only you and I know which magazine's profit margin has dropped."

Liam's stomach plunged as if he'd gone over the hill of a steep roller-coaster. His gaze shot to his laptop on the dresser. Something about it niggled at him.

His neck prickled a warning. "What do you mean *my* numbers?"

"To have *Pulse* publicly humiliated this way is beyond acceptable." Outrage flattened Patrick's voice into monotone. Liam could picture his grandfather talking through clenched teeth. "Do you realize the damage you've done by sharing those numbers prematurely? This is potentially disastrous for EPH as well as highly embarrassing. We needed to release the data on our terms and with the proper spin or we could lose advertising dollars and credibility."

"I didn't leak the information, Patrick."

"Then you'd better ask your lover who did."

Liam looked at Aubrey sitting up in bed and clutching the sheet to her breasts. Concern and curiosity darkened her eyes. He hit the mute button on the phone. "Did you use my laptop yesterday?"

Her brow pleated with confusion. "No. When did I have the time? Why?"

Possibilities tumbled through his mind. When indeed? Aubrey had been with him all day, even when he showered. Besides, they'd been out of the house most of the day. And then he remembered the woman he'd thought to be a member of the household staff he hadn't met heading toward their bedroom yesterday. Aubrey might not have stolen the data on his computer, but one of her father's minions had both motive and opportunity.

He unmuted the phone. "I didn't leak the information, but I'm staying at Holt's house in Napa Valley. Someone here could have accessed my laptop and stolen the file."

Beside him Aubrey gasped.

Patrick swore. "That's exactly the kind of underhanded trick that bastard would try. When you sleep in the enemy's viper pit, Liam, you open yourself up to his bite. I hope like hell your choice hasn't done irreparable damage to EPH."

His grandfather disconnected with a slam. Liam closed and slowly lowered his phone and then swore.

"What happened?"

"Your father had someone steal files off my computer."

"What?" She gaped in disbelief.

"Today's newspaper printed confidential EPH accounting

files. Files I had on my laptop. I didn't submit them and neither did anyone else at EPH."

"You think my father would do something that despicable?"

"Yes."

"How dare you!"

"Yesterday morning I angled my laptop away from the window so I could read my e-mail without the early morning light glaring on the screen. Today my computer is facing the window. If you didn't use it, then somebody else did."

Doubt clouded her eyes. "M-maybe the maid shifted it when she dusted."

"You can ask, but what you're going to discover is that your father had one of his flunkies hack into my computer, steal my file and turn it over to the *Times*. The question is whether or not you knew what he planned and kept me out of the house to facilitate the process."

She flinched. Wide-eyed and pale, she climbed from the bed, dragging the sheet with her. "I can't believe you said that. You said you loved me. And now you have the audacity to suggest I'd help my father hurt you? You can't love someone you don't trust, Liam."

He raked a hand over his face. Did he suspect Aubrey? Not really, but the doubt had been planted, spreading its roots through him like a poisonous, choking vine. Was Aubrey just one more example of his habit of choosing the wrong women?

"Has your father ever asked you about EPH?" Her gulp and the nervous flutter of her lashes as she looked away gave him the answer he needed. Tension knotted his neck and dread twisted his gut. He had a question to ask, one to which he knew damned well he didn't want to know the answer. "Did you schedule our first meeting to squeeze me for information, Aubrey?"

Her hand clenched by her side and guilt filled her expression. Pain knifed Liam from all sides. Damn, he'd been a stupid, gullible fool.

"Yes, but you didn't tell me anything, and then after what happened between us, I couldn't…" She lifted her chin. "I tried to say goodbye, Liam, but you wouldn't let me. You sent flowers and you called. And then we promised to keep our business and personal lives separate. We made rules."

As if making rules kept people from breaking them. Had Aubrey played him for a fool? Had she betrayed him the same way Patrick had, by using information Liam had shared in confidence to hurt his family? Or was she telling the truth? He needed space to find the answers, and he needed to get back to New York and start damage control—if he still had a job.

"Liam, you have to believe me. I would never deliberately hurt you."

"I'm going home."

"I understand. I'll start pack—"

"Alone."

She staggered back a step, pressing a hand to her chest. Resignation settled over her features. "Fine. Go. I told you this wouldn't last, but I expected your promise to hold for more than a few hours."

She retreated to the bathroom and closed the door. Why did the quiet click feel like a nail in his heart?

Shaking with a tangle of emotions she couldn't even begin to separate and identify, Aubrey hammered on her father's apartment door.

When he didn't open immediately, she pounded again. She knew he was at home. The doorman had verified it when she'd asked on her way up. Finally, the door opened, revealing her father in his bathrobe. She'd never known him to go to bed before midnight. It was only nine.

"Aubrey, I thought you were in California."

"I came here straight from the airport." She shouldered past him and into the den. The remnants of Chinese takeout littered the coffee table, along with two glasses. Two plates. He wasn't alone. Was the woman waiting in his bedroom? Not a road Aubrey wanted to travel. She'd suspected he had women since divorcing her mother, but she'd never been confronted with the evidence. That he had someone now when she was alone seemed like a mocking twist of fate.

If she weren't furious and a little afraid that Liam's accusations might possibly have a grain of truth to them, she'd excuse herself and talk to her father tomorrow. But she'd repeatedly replayed this morning's encounter during the seven-hour flight home, debating both sides of the situation.

Liam was wrong. He had to be. She'd get the proof and then... What? Liam didn't trust her. Didn't that say it all? Love didn't stand a chance without trust. But she had to know if Liam's doubts were well-founded or if he'd just been looking for a way to end their relationship.

"Aubrey, this isn't a good time."

"Did you have someone hack into Liam Elliott's computer and steal his files?"

Something flashed in her father's eyes, but it vanished before she could interpret it. "It's late. I have company. We can discuss this tomorr—"

His evasiveness made her shift uneasily. "Did you?"

He folded his arms and set his chin in that stubborn my-way-or-the-highway expression she'd come to know so well, and Aubrey's heart sank. She silently shrieked, No!

"I asked you to get the information and you didn't. The report you requested from the sales team was a good start, but—"

"I deleted that report."

"All files are backed up on our e-mail server. You know that.

You should have brought the report to me, Aubrey. It's your job."

Her job to betray someone who trusted her? Nausea rose in her throat. Anger, pain, betrayal and guilt whirled through her like debris in a tornado. "How could you?"

"We needed the competitive edge the information could give us. It's business, Aubrey."

"It's my life! It's the man I love." As soon as she said it she knew it was true. What she felt for Liam wasn't infatuation. Infatuation wouldn't hurt this much. She wanted to crawl in a dark hole and tend to her wounds. She wanted to strike out at her father and at herself for her part in the whole sordid disaster.

How unfair that she'd discover that she loved Liam Elliott now when it was too late.

Her father's scowl deepened. "I assigned you a job. I never intended for you to get personally involved with Elliott."

"No, you intended to get what you wanted regardless of the casualties, and as usual you bulldozed over any*thing* and any*one* in your path. This time it was me, Dad."

He lifted a shoulder as if to say, "So?"

"You know everything there is to know about running Holt Enterprises, but you don't know anything about being a father."

He flinched. "This is not about being a father. This is bus—"

"No, Dad, I'm going to say my piece and for once you're going to listen. I didn't want a new sports car every two years. I didn't want expensive jewelry or designer clothing. All I wanted was time with you to prove that I was just as good as the son you wanted but never had. All I wanted was a father who loved me and one who would say so. Just once."

She hated the telling tremor racking her body. She hated the tears streaming down her cheeks even more and angrily swiped them away. Both were signs of weakness and Matthew Holt didn't tolerate weakness.

A muscle ticked in her father's jaw and he swallowed. He opened his mouth, but Aubrey halted his words with an upraised hand.

"I can't work for someone I no longer trust, someone who would deliberately use me and hurt me in some selfish quest to become number one. I quit. I'll clean out my office this weekend, and I'll be out of my apartment as soon as possible. I refuse to be your pawn any longer." She headed for the front door before she completely broke down, but then paused, took a bracing breath and turned back.

"I want Hill Crest and I want it now. Gram's will said it would be deeded to me when I married, but thanks to your greed and your lack of scruples the only man I've ever wanted to marry will probably never speak to me again."

Her father's lips thinned, but otherwise he displayed no emotion. Did he realize the wreck he'd made of her life? Did he even care? "I'll take care of it."

Aubrey's fingers closed around the doorknob.

"Aubrey." His gruff voice stopped her. "I never thought you'd be hurt."

She swallowed the sob rising in her throat, opened the door and looked over her shoulder at her father. "No, Dad, you never thought of me at all. That's what I'm talking about."

"Liam, Aubrey Holt to see you," Ann said from his open door.

Everything in Liam flashed cold and then hot and then cold again. After the weekend he'd had butting heads with Patrick, soothing family members and working with the PR team to formulate a damage control plan, the last thing he wanted was to start his Monday off by dealing with the one crisis he hadn't faced. The one he'd deliberately blocked every waking moment. But damn, Aubrey had haunted his dreams.

"I'm busy. Tell her to make an appoint—"

"Liam," Aubrey said from behind Ann's shoulder, "please."

Damn. Double damn. If somebody took a dull knife and cut out his heart it would probably hurt less than seeing Aubrey. He clenched his molars and jerked his chin, indicating for Ann to leave them. His assistant stepped aside for Aubrey to enter and then pulled the door closed behind her.

Aubrey looked like hell, as if she hadn't had any more sleep than he'd had since he'd left her on Friday. The circles smudging the pale skin beneath her eyes were almost the same deep purple as her eyes. Her black pinstriped suit and stark white shirt didn't help.

What is she wearing under there? The question struck as swift as a rattlesnake. *No longer your business, Elliott.*

He didn't stand, didn't offer her a seat. Rude of him, but he didn't owe her any politeness. Besides, if he stood he might lose the battle against the need to take her in his arms. Aubrey was part of his past. Just one more woman on his list of poorly chosen lovers.

Their relationship was over. Finished. Done.

Damn.

He sat back in his leather desk chair and folded his arms across his chest. "What do you want, Aubrey?"

Fisting her hands by her side, she inhaled slowly, deeply, and shifted in her sensible black pumps. "I came to apologize. You were right. My father did have someone go through your computer."

Hearing her confirm what he already knew didn't repair the damage. "Fine, you've apologized. Goodbye."

Instead of heading out the door she took a step closer to his desk. "When my father found out about us, he told me he wanted me to be happy. I had no idea he was setting me up so he could use me to get to you and to EPH through you. I want you to know that I don't condone what he did, and I didn't have anything to do with his plan, Liam."

She took another step forward. "You're also right about our first meeting. I did set it up to try and pry information out of you, but that job ended before we made love. Anything you told me after that I kept to myself.

"After the ball, my father pressed me to find out more about what was causing so much turmoil at EPH. I asked the sales team to milk our mutual advertisers for any rumors they may have heard about the shake-up at EPH. The advertising sales manager compiled a report and sent it to me. But I destroyed it, Liam. I couldn't forward that information to my father because I was falling in love with you. Even though it was commonly known gossip I knew it might hurt you.

"My father found the report anyway. I don't know if that's what spurred him into hiring someone to hack into your computer or if cyber-snooping was already part of his plan. It doesn't really matter. What matters is that I was trying so hard to impress him that I compromised my integrity. I'm ashamed of my part in this mess and I'm sorry you were hurt."

He steeled himself against the tremor of her voice, but it got to him and that pissed him off. "Are you done yet?"

"No. One more thing… I love you."

He sucked in a sharp breath at the unexpected jab.

"And it's not the transient kind of infatuation my mother fell in and out of on a regular basis. I *love* you. I love your smile, your patience, your enthusiasm and your loyalty to your family. I love the way you make me feel like the sexiest woman in the world and how you made me feel loved for the first time in my life." Her lips quivered. "And I'll never forget the happiness you've given me in the past few weeks. Thank you for that."

The knot in his throat nearly choked him. He couldn't speak and he could barely breathe.

"But I also know we can't get past this because of your loyalty to your family and my misplaced loyalty to mine. Goodbye, Liam. Be happy."

She left him clutching the arms of his chair in a white-knuckled grip and fighting the burn in his gut and the one in his eyes.

"Do you want to tell us why you called this 'urgent' meeting?" Gannon, Liam's oldest brother, asked as he sat down at the long table in the EPH executive boardroom on the twenty-fourth floor.

The sun shining in from the rooftop garden didn't lighten Liam's mood. He waited for Tag, his younger brother, and Bridget, his sister, to take their seats before sitting or replying. "I wanted to personally apologize for the leak to the *Times*. I screwed up."

Gannon snorted. "No kidding."

Defense surged hot and fast through Liam. He tamped it down. As executive editor of *Pulse,* Gannon had been the hardest hit by Holt's devious attack. Tag, *Pulse*'s news editor, came in a close second.

Aubrey's confession and apology from earlier that morning whirled round and round in Liam's head. "I left my laptop where I shouldn't have. I was careless. It won't happen again."

Tag leaned forward, lacing his fingers and bracing his arms on the table. "Did you suspect a setup?"

"No." Should he have? It was a question he'd asked himself over and over and over. Dammit, if only he and Aubrey had stayed at a hotel. Or would something like this have happened eventually anyway? Had Matthew Holt tagged Liam as the weak link at EPH? As Patrick said, Liam had made himself available for the enemy to use.

Tag shrugged. "If you didn't suspect anything, then I don't see how this screwup is your fault. Holt's a bastard. We all know that. Getting involved with his daughter probably isn't the smartest move you've ever made, but you're not known for making stupid moves, Liam. I'm betting there's a pretty good reason."

Liam snorted at that. Every woman he'd ever hooked up with had been a mistake. "I didn't know who Aubrey was when we met, and she…she blew me away. I've never been that attracted to a woman before. But I should have said goodbye as soon as I learned her name."

But then he wouldn't have gotten to know Aubrey, wouldn't have had the chance to find peace in her presence or ecstasy in her arms. He couldn't honestly say he regretted his time with her. In fact, even knowing the painful end, if he had to do it all over again, he would. But he'd leave his laptop at home.

"Do you love her?" asked Bridget, who had remained silent until this point.

Liam exhaled slowly and considered the question he'd refused to ask himself since Aubrey had walked out two hours ago. "Yes."

Would he get over his feelings, the way Aubrey predicted? He didn't think so.

His little sister moved in for the kill. Liam recognized the glint in her eyes and the shift in her posture. Her recent marriage to a Colorado sheriff and distance from EPH had softened Bridget in many ways, but it hadn't diminished her energetic roll-up-the-sleeves-and-dive-in personality. He was happy she was here for a visit; he'd missed her. "Do you think she knew what her father had planned?"

"At first I thought she did. Now I know better. Aubrey didn't set me up. She came by to apologize this morning." Without a doubt she'd told the truth today. He'd seen the honesty and pain in her eyes. She'd been duped by her bastard of a father, and Matthew Holt's actions had cut her deeply. Liam's heart ached for her. He knew how much betrayal by someone you loved and trusted hurt.

Is cutting her out of your life any less of a betrayal?
You promised to make your relationship work.

He stifled his conscience and dealt with the facts. "But Aubrey admitted to asking Holt Enterprises' sales reps to quiz our mutual advertisers and then report any rumors about EPH. She said she tore up the report, but that Holt found it anyway. I could never be certain that kind of encroachment wouldn't happen again. Aubrey's trying so damned hard to prove her worth to her father that I'd always have to watch my back and my tongue for fear the next time she heard insider information about EPH she wouldn't discard it."

"So you love her. What are you going to do about it?" Bridget asked.

What could he do? "Nothing."

"Nothing?" his siblings chorused in unison.

"What choice do I have? Aubrey's right. As long as she works for Holt and I work for EPH we can't get past this. We'd each be an enemy and a potential spy in the other's family camp, especially after this. We're a modern-day Romeo and Juliet, for God's sake. There is no happy ending."

Tag shook his head. "If you love her, you'll find a way to make it work. Ending a relationship because it's going to be difficult is just another form of cowardice."

Tag ought to know. His fiancée was African-American. The couple hadn't let racial differences and fear of prejudice wreck their love. It hadn't been easy.

Gannon laid a hand on Liam's shoulder. "If you really love this woman, learn from your big brother's mistakes. I let concern for what others might say break up Erika and me the first time around, and I almost lost the best woman I've ever met. Don't make that mistake. You might not get a second chance like I did."

Confused, Liam looked from one sibling to the other. "Her part in this doesn't bother you?"

"It sounds as if she was used as much as you were," Gannon replied. "As much as I hated having *Pulse*'s numbers exposed, it sounds as if we were all victims of Matthew Holt."

"Aubrey and I couldn't continue to work for rival firms, and I don't think she's willing to give up on winning her father's approval yet."

"Could you be happy working outside EPH? Family duty's always been your mantra."

Tag's question wasn't an easy one. "I don't know. Frankly, Patrick's challenge has made life a living hell around here. Most days I feel like the grim reaper. Good news for one of you is bad news for the other. It's been a lose-lose situation." He scraped a hand over his face. "Jeez, I sound like I'm whining."

"No, little brother, you sound like the pressure of being caught in the middle is finally getting to you."

Liam looked at Gannon. "Being the middle man isn't the only problem. You all know Patrick and I work out and play golf together. I have to wonder if something *I* said didn't spark his idiotic competition. At the very least I should have seen this crazy scheme coming and headed it off. Patrick swears he's doing this to make EPH stronger, but he's tearing the family apart."

Bridget rolled her eyes. "Who knows where Patrick's crazy scheme came from. But you're not responsible for his actions,

Liam, and you can't let his interference ruin your life." She held up her hands. "I know, I know, you've all heard that from me for years, but from the vantage point of Colorado, I look back on my time here and I see how hard we all tried to please him and to follow his rules. I'm over my need to embarrass him with a tell-all Elliott exposé, but the point is Patrick has had too much control over our choices and our lives. You have to do what makes *you* happy, Liam. It's *your* life. You'll have to live it long after he's gone."

Tag nodded. "I'll second that."

"I concur," said Gannon.

Bridget sat forward. "Liam, you're a great problem solver. If anyone can come up with an acceptable compromise it's you."

Touched by his siblings' support, Liam took a fortifying breath. "So all I have to do is find a solution that makes everybody happy. A piece of cake."

Not.

Eleven

Liam entered Patrick's office without knocking. "Aubrey wasn't part of Holt's scheme."

His grandfather looked up from the reports on his desk. "Are you certain of that?"

"Yes. Patrick, I'm in love with her, and I need to know if you can get past your enmity with her father or if my relationship with Aubrey will be a source of friction."

"And if I can't get past it?"

Liam took a deep breath. He'd thought long and hard since talking to his siblings. Lunch sat like a bed of hot coals in his stomach. He needed Aubrey in his life and he had to find a way to make it work. "Then I'll tender my resignation."

Patrick didn't look surprised, but, after losing three other family employees this year, maybe he wasn't. He laid his favorite Montblanc pen on his desk. His leather chair creaked as he sat back. "And do what? Start a winery in California?"

Liam drew a sharp breath. "I don't know."

"Do you think I haven't seen your books, Liam? Do you think I don't know that while your head is here at EPH your heart is elsewhere?"

Insulted, Liam bristled. "I've given one hundred percent to EPH even though I have to admit that in the past ten months I haven't enjoyed my role here."

"I know that, but I have my reasons for seeing this competition through."

Liam didn't waste his time trying to decipher Patrick's riddle. He'd done that for ten months and failed. "I want to marry Aubrey if she'll have me. If she won't quit her job, then I'll have to quit mine. If you can't accept her into the family and absolve her in this, then I'll have to quit anyway."

"Only you can make the decision about which is more important—the woman or the job."

"What kind of vague nonanswer is that?"

Patrick lifted his pen. "The only one you're going to get from me. If you'll excuse me, I have work to do."

No closer to resolving his dilemma than he'd been hours ago, Liam let himself out of the office. Something had to give. His job? Or Aubrey? Could he be happy without either?

And was it a moot question? Would Aubrey give him a second chance or tell him to go to hell for breaking his promise at the first hurdle?

Another bitch of a day. The good news was it was almost over and it couldn't get worse. Liam pulled open the glass front door to his apartment building. "Evening, Carlos."

"Evening, Mr. Elliott. You have a visitor." The doorman nodded toward the corner of the lobby. Liam whipped his head sideways, hoping to find Aubrey. Instead he saw her father, Matthew Holt, rising from the sofa.

Liam's hand tightened on his briefcase. After the day he'd had he did not need this aggravation. "Holt, I have nothing to say to you."

"Then listen."

"Forget it." Liam headed for his elevator. Holt followed.

"It's about Aubrey."

Liam's step hitched, but he kept moving. He wanted a glass of wine. Hell, who was he kidding? He wanted a shot of whiskey. Maybe three shots.

"She quit her job and she's moving out of her apartment."

That stopped him. Liam turned. His heart slammed against his ribs with the force of a jackhammer wrecking a concrete sidewalk. "What?"

"She called me a selfish bastard. And she's right."

Liam studied Holt's drawn face. The man looked decades older than the photos Liam usually saw in the paper. "Upstairs."

The elevator opened instantly. Liam waited for Holt to precede him. Seconds later he let the enemy into his home. Bad decision? Probably. Would he regret it? That remained to be seen. "What happened?"

"Aubrey came by my place as soon as she returned from California Friday night. She chewed me out for using her as a pawn and for hurting her and the man she loves."

An invisible steel band compressed Liam's chest. "She should have punched you."

Holt nodded. "I would have deserved it. She's leaving New York."

Another hit, this one winding Liam. He crossed to the wet bar, set down his briefcase and poured himself a glass of Woodford Reserve whiskey. He poured a second for his unwanted visitor. The bite of the liquor only added to the burn in his belly. "When did she quit?"

"Friday night."

Why hadn't she told him when she'd come to see him that morning? Was it because it didn't matter? Because she didn't want to be with him now? "And you're telling me all this because…?"

Holt downed half his liquor in one gulp. "Because Aubrey won't answer my calls or open her door, and because I've damaged my relationship with my daughter beyond repair. I don't want to be responsible for doing the same to her relationship with you." He knocked back the last of his drink. "I'm a selfish son of a bitch, Elliott, and I won't be a bargain in the father-in-law department, but I want Aubrey to be happy. Apparently, you make her happy."

Liam had made her happy. *Had* being the operative word. And she'd made him happy, happier than he'd ever been. But then he'd hurt her with his lack of trust and his unjust accusations. Holt's relationship with Aubrey might not be the only irreparable one.

But she loved him. Or at least she had. And God knows he loved her. Burying himself in work eighteen hours a day hadn't helped. Not a second had passed since Friday that he hadn't ached for her. He couldn't walk away without trying to salvage the bond they'd forged.

He set his glass aside. "I'll call her."

"She won't answer. I don't know how in the hell to get through to her."

"I'll find a way." He had to.

"Elliott, if you get through, would you tell her…tell her I'm sorry and that I love her?" Defeat curved Holt's shoulders.

"I'll tell her, but she needs to hear it from you."

Liam closed the door behind Holt. He had to have a plan, a

foolproof plan, to regain Aubrey's love and trust before she left New York. Before he lost her completely. If he hadn't already.

The barrier of her job no longer stood between them. That was a start, but was it enough?

"Happy Halloween, ma'am," the courier said before departing.

"You, too," Aubrey replied automatically, her gaze stuck on the envelope in her hand. The return address read Ernie's Pub. *Liam*. Her heart hesitated and then settled into a heavy *thud-thud*. She closed her door and walked blindly back into her apartment and tripped over a box.

She caught herself against the wall and surveyed the room. Packing boxes littered the floor and tabletops. Uneasiness slithered through her. Moving was the right thing to do. Wasn't it? She couldn't stay here knowing that her father was a jerk without scruples and that Liam lived just around the corner.

Liam. Her gaze returned to the envelope and a well of ache opened up inside her. He thought she'd betrayed him. That he could believe her capable of such deceit didn't just hurt. It angered her. She dumped the envelope, unopened, into a nearby trash can and returned to the kitchen and her packing.

Think positively, A. You'll finally get a chance to open your bed-and-breakfast.

Yesterday after talking to Liam she'd come home, cried until her eyes had practically swollen shut, and then she'd picked up the phone and called Jared Maxwell, the B&B owner she'd met in California. Mason's brother-in-law had generously agreed to walk through Hill Crest House with Aubrey and to guide her in setting up business. By this time next year Aubrey would be an innkeeper. The thought didn't fill her with the happiness she'd expected.

She'd miss Liam. The unexpected thought slipped through

her defenses, renewing her anger. She slammed pots and pans into a box. How could he think she'd betray him?

Because his grandfather had.

Her hands slowed. Liam had already been hurt by someone he loved and trusted, and from what little he'd let slip about his relationship with his grandfather the wound was open and raw. What else would he expect except that she'd betray him, too?

Her anger evaporated. Aubrey set the vegetable steamer on the counter and returned to the trash can. Open the envelope or not? Heartache either way. She retrieved the envelope and ripped it open. Inside she found a bright or-ange-and-black flier from Ernie's Pub advertising its Hallow-een party tonight.

"Costumes preferred, but not required. Seven to midnight, the witching hour."

Liam's handwriting in the margin caught her eye.

"I wouldn't wear this getup for anyone else. Please come. Liam."

Her heart pounded and her mouth dried. She clutched the flier to her chest and tried to tamp down the hope rising inside her like a hot air balloon. Liam wanted to see her. Why? She reread the note, looking for a clue in the short sentences, but found none.

Getup? He'd be in costume?

Should she go?

No.

Yes. What did she have to lose? She'd already lost her heart.

She glanced at the clock. Three hours to find a costume. Most likely an impossible task on Halloween night.

* * *

"You okay in there?" Pam, the waitress, asked as she set Liam's drink on the table.

"I'll never eat another sardine," Liam muttered and shifted his shoulders. The accompanying scrape of metal against metal grated on his overstretched nerves. He lifted the tumbler and then set it back down. How in the hell was he supposed to drink it through this helmet?

"Want a flexible straw?"

"I guess I need one. What time is it?" He couldn't fit a watch under his costume.

"Almost nine. You think she'll show?"

The sinking sensation in the pit of Liam's stomach said no, but he refused to give up. Aubrey had been late once before and she'd been worth every second of the wait. He shrugged and his hinges screeched. "We have a few more hours."

Pam patted his shoulder. *Clank. Clank.* "Just give me the signal when you're ready."

He peeled the paper from his straw, stabbed it into the tumbler and lifted his visor to sip. Around him revelers enthusiastically celebrated Halloween in a variety of costumes from common to absurd. His suit of armor fit right in.

He occupied the booth he and Aubrey had used when they'd first met. When he'd arrived, he'd had to bribe the guys who'd occupied it to get them to move, but he figured having the good luck seat when Aubrey arrived was worth a pitcher of beer.

The pub's door opened. His heart had quit stalling each time someone new entered about forty patrons ago. A hooker in a cheap blond wig with a red mask covering the upper half of her face hesitated on the threshold. Her minuscule red halter top cupped small breasts, and a matching miniskirt stretched low on slim hips, leaving a lot of bare skin in between. A navel ring glinted on her flat belly. She'd strapped mile-high heels to her feet.

Wolf whistles and catcalls greeted her. A couple of guys pulled cash out of their wallets and shouted offers. Her neck and the visible part of her face turned almost as red as her clothing. Liam was about to look away when the woman moved forward, looking left and right, searching the patron's faces without looking too closely or acknowledging their lewd invitations. Something about the way the hooker moved looked familiar. His pulse kicked into high gear, and his glass hit the table with a thud. Aubrey.

Sliding out of the booth was as laborious as wedging himself into it had been. He stepped in front of her when she tried to pass. The startled violet eyes looking up at him through the red mask stole his breath.

Her eyes widened in recognition and her lips parted. "A knight in shining armor. It suits you, Liam."

He smiled, but realized she probably couldn't see his mouth. Liam pried off the heavy helmet and set it on the table. "A hooker?"

"I had trouble finding a costume. I was about to give up and come without one, because this is so not me. It's—"

"The sexiest thing I've ever seen." He was as hard as steel beneath his metal suit, and hot. Oh, man, was he hot. He lifted a hand to touch her face, but stopped. The heavy glove would scrape her skin.

"I wouldn't wear this getup for anyone else," Aubrey parroted his words back at him.

"Good to know." He could spend all day looking at her. Aubrey had a body made for sexy clothing. But her delectable body wasn't the reason he'd sent her the bar flier. He gestured to the table instead. "I'm glad you came. Have a seat before I have to draw my sword and start hacking these guys down one by one."

She scooted into the booth, nibbled her siren red lip and studied his face. "I almost didn't come. Why did you send the invitation?"

He grimaced and yanked off his gloves so he could cover her hand with his. "Because I wanted to apologize. Aubrey, I'm sorry. For doubting you. For hurting you. For letting our families come between us. And I'm sorry for breaking my promise. It won't happen again."

"You had good reason."

"I had a good reason to be angry with your father, but not with you." He stroked a thumb over her palm. She shivered and her nipples beaded in the skimpy top. He drew courage from the knowledge that she couldn't be over him when his touch could still turn her on.

"Liam, you told me enough about your grandfather and the situation at work for me to figure out that you believed someone else you loved had betrayed you."

He shouldn't be surprised that she'd figured him out. Aubrey understood him better than anyone. Better than he understood himself, in fact.

"The tension at work, my mother's cancer and my brothers and sister finding someone special to share their lives with made me look hard at my life. Life was passing me by until I met you, Aubrey, and now I'm not only living it I'm looking beyond robotically doing what's expected of me." He caught Pam's eye and thumped the metal breast plate over his heart—their signal. And then he gently removed Aubrey's mask and laid it on the table beside his helmet.

"When we were in Napa you suggested I quit my job at EPH and follow my dream of opening a winery. I rejected your idea because I didn't have the courage to risk it. But you were right. Without risks there are no rewards."

Pam arrived. She slid a silver platter onto the center of the table and quickly departed. On the platter lay a single red rose and a ring box.

Aubrey gasped. Her wide gaze jumped from the tray to Liam's eyes and back again.

Liam lifted the rose and dragged the bud along Aubrey's cheek. "One rose because for one month you've excited me, soothed me and made me happier than anyone ever has. You've made me believe that dreams can come true, Aubrey."

He laid the rose back on the tray, picked up the Tiffany ring box and opened it to reveal a marquise diamond flanked by two heart-shaped amethyst stones. "One flawless diamond because you're more precious to me than anything, and my love for you is as strong and as enduring as this stone. Two amethysts hearts because our hearts belong together and because I've found my destiny in your violet eyes."

He extracted the ring from the box and held out his hand. "I want to spend the rest of my life loving you, Aubrey Holt. Marry me. Please."

His heart stalled when she knotted her fingers and lowered her hands into her lap. "How can you forgive my father for what he's done?"

"I may not ever approve of his business practices, but I'm working on forgiveness because he loves you, and anyone who loves you can't be all bad."

Aubrey made a noise of disgust. "He doesn't love me."

"He came to see me, and trust me, sweetheart, he knows he screwed up. He's sorry and he's hurting and he wants to apologize. I know you're as mad as hell at him now, but he loves you and you love him. Give him a chance to make things right. Families are forever. Remember telling me that?"

Aubrey mashed her trembling lips together. A tear slid down her cheek. "You weren't kidding when you said you're the Elliott peacemaker."

"I just like happy endings. Let me be your knight in shining armor, Aubrey. Let's live out our fantasies and dreams together. Let me make giving you a happily-ever-after my life's crusade."

"What about your job? You'll regret leaving EPH once Patrick's competition is over and life returns to normal."

"No, I won't. We both need jobs that fulfill us, jobs that reward us with more than a paycheck. We're not getting that here. I'd like to stay at EPH through the end of the year to ease the transition, but in the meantime, I want to start looking for a place for us in Napa Valley. A place where you can run your B&B and I can tinker with my grapes. Money's not an issue. I'll net a bundle from selling my apartment, and I have some healthy investments to tide us over until we make a profit."

She searched his face as if waiting for the catch and then a smile flickered on her lips. "I already have the perfect place. Hill Crest House is mine. My grandmother left it to me. There's enough land for you to build your winery, and you can keep your apartment so we have somewhere to stay when we come back to visit our families."

Liam's lungs seized and his pulse took off at a sprinter's pace. "Is that a yes?"

Aubrey lifted her hands and cupped his face. "I love you, Liam Elliott, and nothing would make me happier than being your wife."

He covered her hand with his and then pulled it off his cheek. He held her gaze as he slid the ring on her finger. "I love you, Aubrey Holt, and I swear to you you'll never regret saying yes."

The bar patrons erupted in a cheer and Liam realized they'd had an audience. He pried himself out of the booth, snatched Aubrey into his arms and covered her smiling lips with his.

Fantasies did come true. He ought to know. He'd found his when the enemy's daughter had stormed his castle and captured his heart.

* * * * *

THE ELLIOTTS *continues next month with*
THE EXPECTANT EXECUTIVE
by Kathie Denosky.

A special treat for you from Harlequin Blaze!

Turn the page for a sneak preview of
DECADENT
by
New York Times *bestselling author*
Suzanne Forster

On sale November, 2006
wherever series books are sold.

Harlequin Blaze—Your ultimate destination
for red-hot reads.
With six titles every month, you'll never guess
what you'll discover under the covers...

Run, Ally! Don't be fooled by him. He's evil. Don't let him touch you!

But as the forbidding figure came through the mists toward her, Ally knew she couldn't run. His features burned with dark malevolence, and his physical domination of everything around him seemed to hold her like a net.

She'd heard the tales. She knew all about the Wolverton legend and the ghost that haunted The Willows, an elegant old mansion lost by Micha Wolverton nearly a hundred years ago. According to folklore, the estate was stolen from the Wolvertons, and Micha was killed, trying to reclaim it. His dying vow was to be reunited with the spirit of his beloved wife, who'd taken her life for reasons no one would speak of, except in whispers. But Ally had never put much stock in the fantasy. She didn't believe in ghosts.

Until now—

She still didn't understand what was happening. The figure had materialized out of the mist that lay thick on the damp cemetery soil. A cool breeze and silvery moonlight had played against the ancient stone of the crypts surrounding her, until they joined the mist, causing his body to thicken and solidify right before her eyes. That was when she realized she'd seen this man before. Or thought she had, at least.

His face was familiar. . . so familiar, yet she couldn't put it together. Not with him looming so near. She stepped back as he approached.

"Don't be afraid," he said. His voice wasn't what she expected. It didn't sound as if it were coming from beyond the grave. It was deep and sensual. Commanding.

"Who are you?" she managed.

"You should know. You summoned me."

"No, I didn't." She had no idea what he was talking about. Two minutes ago, she'd been crouching behind a moss-covered crypt, spying on the mansion that had once been The Willows, but was now Club Casablanca. And then this—

If he was Micah, he might be angry that she was trespassing on his property. "I'll go," she said. "I won't come back. I promise."

"You're not going anywhere."

Words snagged in her throat. "Wh-why not? What do you want?"

"If I wanted something, Ally, I'd take it. This is about need."

His words resonated as he moved within inches of her. She tried to back away, but her feet were useless. "And you need something from me?"

"Good guess." His tone burned with irony. "I need lips, soft and surrendered, a body limp with desire."

"My lips, my bod—?"

"Only yours."

"Why? Why me?" This couldn't be Micha. He didn't want any woman but Rose. He'd died trying to get back to her.

"Because you want that, too," he said.

Wanted what? A ghost of her own? She'd always found the legend impossibly romantic, but how could he have known that? How could he know anything about her? Besides, she'd sworn off inappropriate men, and what could be more inappropriate than a ghost? She shook her head again, still not willing to admit the truth. But her heart wouldn't play along. It clattered inside her chest. The mere thought of his kiss, his touch, terrified her. This wildness, it was fear, wasn't it?

When his fingertips touched her cheek, she flinched, expecting his flesh to be cold, lifeless. It was anything but that. His skin was smooth and hot, gentle, yet demanding. And while his dark brown eyes were filled with mystery and wonder, there was a sensitivity about them that threatened to disarm her if she looked too deeply.

"These lips are mine," he said, as if stating a universal fact that she was helpless to avoid. In truth, it was just that. She couldn't stop him.

And she didn't want to.

Find out how the story unfolds in...
DECADENT
by New York Times *bestselling author*
Suzanne Forster.
On sale November 2006.

Harlequin Blaze—Your ultimate destination
for red-hot reads.
With six titles every month, you'll never guess
what you'll discover under the covers...

Silhouette®

nocturne™

USA TODAY bestselling author

MAUREEN CHILD

ETERNALLY

He was a guardian. An immortal fighter of evil,
out to destroy a demon, and she was his next
target. He knew joining with her would make
him strong enough to defeat any demon.
But the cost might be losing the woman
who was his true salvation.

On sale November, wherever books are sold.

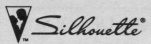

SAVE UP TO $30! SIGN UP TODAY!

INSIDE *Romance*

The complete guide to your favorite
Harlequin®, Silhouette® and Love Inspired® books.

✓ Newsletter ABSOLUTELY FREE! No purchase necessary.

✓ Valuable coupons for future purchases of Harlequin,
   Silhouette and Love Inspired books in every issue!

✓ Special excerpts & previews in each issue. Learn about all
   the hottest titles before they arrive in stores.

✓ No hassle—mailed directly to your door!

✓ Comes complete with a handy shopping checklist
   so you won't miss out on any titles.

- -

SIGN ME UP TO RECEIVE INSIDE ROMANCE
ABSOLUTELY FREE
(Please print clearly)

_____
Name

_____
Address

_____
City/Town   State/Province   Zip/Postal Code

(098 KKM EJL9)

Please mail this form to:
In the U.S.A.: Inside Romance, P.O. Box 9057, Buffalo, NY 14269-9057
In Canada: Inside Romance, P.O. Box 622, Fort Erie, ON L2A 5X3
OR visit http://www.eHarlequin.com/insideromance

IRNBPA06R   ® and ™ are trademarks owned and used by the trademark owner and/or its licensee.

HARLEQUIN®
Blaze™

New York Times bestselling author
Suzanne Forster brings you
another sizzling romance…

Club Casablanca—an exclusive gentleman's club where
exotic hostesses cater to the every need of high-stakes
gamblers, politicians and big-business execs. No rules
apply. And no unescorted women are allowed. Ever.
When a couple gets caught up in the club's hedonistic
allure, the only favors they end up trading are sensual.…

DECADENT

November 2006

by

Suzanne Forster

Get it while it's hot!

Available wherever series romances are sold.

> "Sex and danger ignite a bonfire of passion."
> —*Romantic Times BOOKclub*

REQUEST YOUR FREE BOOKS!

2 FREE NOVELS
PLUS 2
FREE GIFTS!

Passionate, Powerful, Provocative!

COMING NEXT MONTH

#1759 THE EXPECTANT EXECUTIVE—Kathie DeNosky
The Elliotts
An Elliott heiress's unexpected pregnancy is the subject of high-society gossip. Wait till the baby's father finds out!

#1760 THE SUBSTITUTE MILLIONAIRE—Susan Mallery
The Million Dollar Catch
What is a billionaire to do when he discovers the woman he's been hiding his true identity from is carrying his child?

#1761 BEDDED *THEN* WED—Heidi Betts
Marrying his neighbor's daughter is supposed to be merely a business transaction...until he finds himself falling for his convenient wife.

#1762 SCANDALS FROM THE THIRD BRIDE—Sara Orwig
The Wealthy Ransomes
Bought by the highest bidder, a bachelorette has no recourse but to spend the evening with the man who once left her at the altar.

#1763 THE PREGNANCY NEGOTIATION—Kristi Gold
She is desperate to get pregnant. And her playboy neighbor is just the right man for the job.

#1764 HOLIDAY CONFESSIONS—Anne Marie Winston
True love may be blind...but can it withstand the lies between them?